FROM THE
NANCY DREW FILES

THE CASE: Passports have been stolen, and three terrorists are on the loose. Someone on Mykonos —perhaps right in Nancy's hotel—is determined to help them escape.

CONTACT: Zoe Kavalis has invited Nancy to stay at her family's hotel, from which the passports are stolen.

SUSPECTS: Niki Christofouros—Nancy caught the hotel maid rummaging through her bags moments before the passports turned up missing.

Dimitri Zorzis—a professional photographer, he may be the only islander capable of forging the travel documents needed by the terrorists.

Theo Pattakos—he runs a water taxi, and word is he's willing to take anyone anywhere . . . if the price is right.

COMPLICATIONS: Europe has been full of adventure and romance. Nancy and Mick have had a great summer together. But it's time to head home, back to the States . . . and back to Ned.

Books in The Nancy Drew Files® Series

The Nancy Drew Files™

PASSPORT TO ROMANCE #3

Case 74

Greek Odyssey

Carolyn Keene

AN ARCHWAY PAPERBACK
Published by POCKET BOOKS
New York   London   Toronto   Sydney   Tokyo   Singapore

AN ARCHWAY PAPERBACK *Original*

An Archway Paperback published by
POCKET BOOKS, a division of Simon & Schuster Inc.
1230 Avenue of the Americas, New York, NY 10020

ISBN: 0-671-73078-9

First Archway Paperback printing August 1992

10 9 8 7 6 5 4 3 2 1

NANCY DREW, AN ARCHWAY PAPERBACK and colophon
are registered trademarks of Simon & Schuster Inc.

THE NANCY DREW FILES is a trademark
of Simon & Schuster Inc.

Cover art by Tricia Zimic

Printed in the U.S.A.

IL 6+

Chapter

One

"THIS IS EXACTLY what we need," Bess Marvin declared. She combed the water out of her shiny blond hair and adjusted the straps of her red and black polka-dot bikini. "Fun in the sun on one of the most beautiful beaches in the world!"

"Mykonos *is* gorgeous," Nancy Drew agreed, rubbing some sunscreen onto her stomach. The hunter green two-piece suit she was wearing had seemed so daring when she had bought it back in River Heights, but it was tame in comparison to the tiny bikinis worn by most of the other women on the beach.

Tall, athletic George Fayne, Bess's cousin, toweled off her dark curly hair, then flopped down on the sand in her red racing suit. "Didn't I tell you guys you were going to love Greece?" she asked.

1

Greece was the third and final main stop on the girls' summer of traveling in Europe. George had gone ahead early from Rome, joining some Italian teenagers on a trip to Olympia. Nancy, Bess, and Mick Devlin, a cute Australian guy they had met in Geneva, had joined her in Athens the day before. They had arrived on Mykonos late that morning.

Just minutes after checking into the Hotel Athena, the girls had changed into their swimsuits, rushed down the footpath to the beach at the bottom of the hill, and dived into the crystal-clear water. Already Nancy could feel the soothing effect of the golden sun that the Greek islands were so famous for.

With a contented sigh, she took in the panoramic view. Sunlight glittered on the turquoise sea, and sunbathers stretched out on the pastel sand. Off to her left a narrow paved road twisted over rocky terrain until it disappeared into clusters of asymmetrical white houses that made up Chora, the island's main town.

At the top of the hill behind the beach sat the hotel, a square wedding cake of a building, two stories high, with seaside balconies, long wooden shutters, and arched doorways. It was owned and operated by Kostas Kavalis and his daughter, Zoe.

"It was great of Zoe to invite us here," Bess commented, lying back on her towel and closing her eyes. "She seems really nice."

Zoe was a Greek girl whom George had met at Olympia. The two had hit it off, and Zoe had encouraged George to bring her friends to Mykonos for some "Greek hospitality" at her father's inn. When George told Nancy and Bess about her new friend, the girls had decided to spend the last month of their European vacation on Mykonos.

"I knew you'd like her," George said, smiling. She pointed to a speedboat that skittered over the water, pulling a water-skier behind it. "I can't wait to get out there," she said.

Nancy had to admit that the turquoise waters of the Aegean Sea looked inviting. "I'm sure you'll get a chance to water-ski," she said, pushing her reddish gold hair back with a pair of black sunglasses. "We've got a whole month to spend here, and I'm going to kick it off by relaxing— with a capital *R!*"

"I hope that means no more cases," Bess teased. "After the two mysteries you solved in Switzerland and Italy, I think you've done your share of detective work in Europe."

Nancy thought back to the two cases, which she already called *Swiss Secrets* and *Rendezvous in Rome.* "Dealing with blackmailers and jewelry thieves is enough action for one summer," she said, burying her toes in the warm sand. "But you know I can't resist when a mystery comes along—"

She was interrupted by a familiar male voice with an Australian accent. "I think I've died and gone to bikini heaven!"

Smiling, Nancy glanced over to see Mick Devlin coming down the footpath that led to the beach from the hotel. Just the sight of his blond hair and laughing green eyes sent a pleasant tingle racing through her.

Nancy wasn't sure how it had happened, but the gorgeous Australian had found his way deeper and deeper into her heart since she first met him in Switzerland. She hadn't exactly forgotten about Ned Nickerson, her boyfriend back in the States. But she wasn't at all sure where things stood with him, either.

"Have a seat," Nancy said, putting the towel beside her.

"Thanks." Mick peeled off his polo shirt and sprawled in the sand. "Ah . . . this is the life. Hot sun, cool sea, beautiful girl." He gave Nancy's hand a squeeze. "Can't think of any way I'd rather spend a Monday afternoon."

"Well, don't get too cozy," Nancy teased, pulling a book entitled *Let's See Europe* out of her tote bag. "From reading our guidebook, I think the islands will keep us pretty busy."

Mick propped himself up on one elbow to read over her shoulder. "I see what you mean. There's snorkeling, windsurfing, dancing, island-hopping . . ."

"Sounds great!" George put in.

Bess cracked open an eye to look at her friends. "Don't forget, there are shops and marketplaces to scope out, too. I'm dying to check out those quaint little places I saw near the harbor in Chora when our ferry came in."

"I thought you'd given up shopping," Nancy teased, referring to their experience in Rome. In a small shop Bess had inadvertently exchanged her fake Etruscan necklace for a real one, which the girls later learned had been stolen. As a result, their relaxing vacation had turned into a suspenseful search for a jewel thief.

"Oh, that was another time, another country," Bess said airily.

Nancy laughed. "Maybe we can squeeze in some shopping this afternoon," she said, shielding her eyes from the sun. "I don't want to stay out here too long, or I'll be as crisp as a french fry."

Just then a pretty dark-haired girl appeared on the footpath. "Who's ready for lemonade?" Zoe Kavalis asked, holding up a plastic thermos. In her other hand she carried a straw bag with glasses in it.

"Just in the nick of time," George said, jumping up to help Zoe pour. "That swim definitely made me thirsty."

Zoe handed Nancy a glass of lemonade, then paused to push a spray of tiny curls out of her eyes. A tall, fine-boned girl with smooth olive skin and brown eyes, Zoe wore her wavy, dark hair coiled at the nape of her neck.

"I thought I would never make it to the beach!" Zoe said, unbuttoning her sundress to reveal a royal blue one-piece swimsuit.

"We saw that busload of British tourists at the hotel," Nancy said. "Were they checking out—or in?"

"Out, thank goodness!" Zoe said, rolling her eyes in relief. "Papa was happy to have the business, but I was not sorry to see a crowd that size go. Too much work."

In the distance Nancy heard the buzz of an approaching motorboat. She looked out over the water and saw a good-size yellow boat cut in toward the shoreline. Although she couldn't read the Greek letters of the boat's name, she did make out a five-pointed star painted on the bow.

Zoe glanced over, and Nancy saw her frown. "That is Theo Pattakos—he's a fisherman."

The boat swerved to within a few yards of the shore before the young man aboard cut the engine. As he dropped the anchor over the side, Nancy saw that Theo was a solid, muscular guy with black hair that was slicked back off his brow. His bare chest was tanned a golden brown that seemed even darker against his fluorescent orange swim trunks.

He called out a greeting and waved exuberantly to all the sunbathers on the beach. Then he jumped into the water and waded ashore.

"Zoe, my friend!" he called, his arms open wide to give her an affectionate hug.

"Stay away! You're all wet," Zoe said, dodging him. She didn't seem very glad to see him, Nancy noticed. With a tight smile Zoe introduced Nancy, Mick, Bess, and George.

Theo's brown eyes twinkled as he smiled at Nancy and her friends. "Theologos Pattakos, water taxi, tour boat, and fishing boat, at your service. But everyone calls me Theo."

Nancy smiled. "Sounds as if you've got quite a business going, Theo."

He nodded toward his boat. "The *Sea Star* is my first love." He casually slipped an arm around Zoe's shoulders, adding, "Zoe is my second."

"Not anymore," Zoe said, pushing him away. Nancy noticed the brittle tension in Zoe's voice as she went on to explain, "Theo and I *used* to date, but now we're just friends."

There was a story here, Nancy thought, but she didn't want to pry.

"Do you think you can find the time to take George water-skiing?" Zoe asked Theo. "I'll bet she's an excellent water-skier."

George's eyes lit up with excitement. "I'd love to!"

Theo waved toward the boat and smiled. "Let's go!"

Nancy thought he seemed relieved to get away from the tense situation with Zoe. A moment later George and Theo were speeding out to sea aboard the *Sea Star*.

"And now it's time for me to take a dip before I go back to work," Zoe said, starting for the water.

Bess decided to join Zoe, but Nancy and Mick stretched out on the beach and continued to read Nancy's guidebook.

Mick pointed to a small islet just east of Mykonos on the map. "Dragonisi is so close. We've got to see it," he said. "It says here that it's uninhabited and riddled with caves."

"Might be fun to explore," Nancy agreed. "Then there's Naxos, Delos, Tinos . . ." She shook her head as she leafed through the pages. "It's a good thing we've got a month to explore!"

They were checking the boat schedule to Delos, the holy island of the ancient Greeks, when laughter distracted Nancy. She looked up to see Bess and Zoe posing for a roving photographer.

"Wait!" Zoe laughed, rubbing water out of her eyes.

After arranging her slick, wet hair on one shoulder, Bess moved closer to Zoe and flashed the dark-haired photographer a grin. "Okay, shoot," Bess told him.

As soon as the photographer handed the instant photo to Bess, she ran over to Nancy and Mick. "You guys have to get your picture taken, too," Bess insisted, waving the developing photo at them. "My treat." She knelt down on her beach towel and reached into her tote bag for money.

"Such a beautiful couple," the photographer said, focusing his camera on Nancy and Mick.

Mick slipped his arm around Nancy and mugged for the camera. "Say *feta,*" he teased, using the Greek word for goat cheese.

Once the photographer had snapped their picture, Bess paid and thanked him, carefully saying, *"Evcharistó."*

"Parakaló . . . you're welcome," answered the photographer. Nancy guessed that he was in his early twenties. The warm breeze ruffled his curly black hair and crisp white shirt. There was an

appreciative look on his angular face as he gazed at Bess. He definitely seemed interested in her.

"Looks like romance is in the air," Nancy whispered to Mick.

"That's no surprise," he answered with a knowing grin. "Bess has managed to charm half of Europe."

"It's a pleasure to photograph such beautiful people, even if it *is* my job," the photographer told Bess, lingering by Nancy's towel. "I'm Dimitri Zorzis, the *best* photographer on Mykonos. I have a studio in Chora, where I do much better work than this." He gestured at the photos, which were now becoming clear.

"Oh, I don't know," Bess said, studying the picture of Zoe and her. "This is pretty good."

"Because of the subjects, of course," Dimitri insisted, flashing Bess a winning smile. "You are models?"

"No," Bess answered, blushing with pleasure. "Nancy, Mick, and I are just tourists. And Zoe lives here. Her father owns the Hotel Athena."

Dimitri nodded at Zoe, then gave Bess a friendly wink. "Well, I hope you will let me know if you want to capture more of your vacation on film," he said. After slinging his camera over his shoulder, he continued on to the next group of sunbathers.

Bess couldn't take her eyes off Dimitri as he walked along the beach. "Greek guys are so gorgeous," she insisted. "I could stay on this island forever."

Nancy raised an eyebrow at Bess. "From the way Dimitri smiled at you, I don't think he'd mind at all."

"Well, you'll have a chance to meet many Greek people tomorrow night at dinner," Zoe said. "It will be a very special occasion—a celebration of my cousin's engagement. You are all invited to join the festivities."

"Terrific!" Bess exclaimed.

Zoe pulled on her sundress, then picked up the plastic thermos and put the glasses in the straw bag. "I have to get back to the inn. If I can get enough done this afternoon, I'll be free to spend all of tomorrow with you."

Nodding at the guidebook propped open between Nancy and Mick, Zoe asked, "Have you decided what you want to see first?"

"How about Delos?" Nancy said, turning to a page she had marked in the book. "It says here that there's a boat leaving for the island at ten-fifteen each morning."

"Sounds good to me," Bess put in.

Zoe smiled her approval. "You'll like Delos. It is full of statues, mosaics, and marble ruins." She waved at George, who was zipping across the water not far from shore, then picked up the tote bag and started up the hill. "See you at dinner— around nine-thirty," she called. Then she disappeared up the footpath.

"Nine-thirty!" Bess groaned. "By that time I may faint from hunger."

"George warned us that people eat pretty late

here," Nancy said. "But I'm sure we'll find some way to pass the time."

The afternoon sun was just beginning to wane when George finally swam in from water-skiing. Mick wanted to linger on the beach, but the girls decided to head back to the inn to shower and then explore the town of Chora before dinner.

Nancy, Bess, and George were sharing a large, airy suite on the second floor of the hotel. When they checked in, Nancy had been charmed by the balcony view of the sea, the floor-to-ceiling windows with wooden shutters, and the beds covered in crisp white coverlets.

"First one in gets the shower!" Bess called as she turned toward the staircase that led to their room.

"You're on," George agreed, sprinting after her cousin.

All three girls raced up the stairs, but George pushed ahead, reaching the door to their room first. To her surprise it was open.

She stopped short, and Nancy nearly plowed into her. She looked over George's shoulder into the sunny lounge area of their room. "Whoa!" Nancy said under her breath.

A tumbled mess of clothes covered the sofa and wicker chairs. Bess's nightcase was upside down on the floor. Nancy stepped forward and squatted just inches away from a tan puddle near the case. "What's this?"

"My makeup!" Bess gasped, joining Nancy.

A bottle of beige foundation lotion lay splattered on the wooden floor. Beside it sat tangled strings of beads and rhinestones.

"Someone's been in our room," George observed, frowning.

"And they've been going through my luggage," Bess said.

Nancy froze as she heard the sound of running water coming from their bathroom. "Wait a minute," she whispered, motioning for her friends to remain still. Her eyes flew to the bathroom door, which was open a crack.

"We're not alone," Nancy whispered. "Someone's in the bathroom!"

Chapter

Two

ADRENALINE MADE Nancy's heart pound as she peered toward the bathroom. Whoever was in there could be dangerous.

"Come on, Nan!" George whispered, inching out the open door. Bess was already in the hallway.

As Nancy backed away, she got a glimpse of the intruder. It was a girl—a petite brunette with short-cropped straight hair. She was wearing a crisp white uniform with a blue apron. Nancy felt a surge of relief. The girl wasn't a thief—she was a maid!

Taking a step forward, Nancy opened the bathroom door wide. At the same instant the girl shut off the water and turned around. She blanched when she came face-to-face with Nan-

13

cy. "Oh," she gasped, clutching a wet cloth in her hands. "I didn't hear you come in."

Nancy crossed her arms over her chest and stared at the girl. "We weren't expecting maid service, since we just checked in this afternoon."

"Just checked in—yes. Well, welcome to Mykonos." The girl nodded, then walked past Nancy and nervously knelt beside the puddle of spilled makeup. "I'm very sorry about this mess. I bumped into the case, and it fell open."

Nancy watched the maid as she started dabbing at the puddle. From the young woman's red face, Nancy could tell that she was embarrassed. And from the mess in the room, it was obvious to Nancy that the girl hadn't knocked over Bess's luggage. She had been going through it. But why?

George poked her head into the room, surveyed the situation, then joined Nancy.

The maid seemed afraid to look up. She rubbed the wooden floor until not a trace of makeup remained, then said, "I just came to your room to bring you extra towels and some fresh fruit. Zoe wanted her American friends to feel welcome."

Nancy glanced over at the low wooden table. A stack of white towels and a wide bowl filled with oranges, bananas, and grapes sat on the tabletop. "That was nice of Zoe," she said. Then she looked pointedly at the mess on the floor.

The maid began to fumble with the snarled necklaces on the floor.

Bess exchanged a look with Nancy and George,

then bent down to help the maid return the jewelry to the overnight case. "Well, it looks like everything is here and okay. Don't worry about it," she told the girl. "My name is Bess Marvin. And this is Nancy Drew and George Fayne."

"Niki Christofouros," the maid introduced herself, scrambling to her feet and nodding at the girls.

Nancy looked carefully at the girl. She had large black eyes, lined with dark makeup, which gave her a mysterious look. With her high cheekbones and stylish bob, Nancy thought that Niki looked as if she had stepped off the cover of a fashion magazine.

"Thanks for the fruit," Nancy said, deciding not to press the issue. "Tell Zoe that we feel very much at home here."

"Yes, I'll tell her," Niki promised, edging away. Then she disappeared out the door.

George closed the door, then glanced around the room. "What's her problem?"

"She *was* acting strange," Nancy agreed.

Bess was sifting through her open suitcase. "There doesn't seem to be anything missing, but why was she going through my stuff?"

"That's exactly what I was wondering," Nancy said as she sank down onto one of the room's three beds.

"And why just your stuff, Bess?" George wanted to know. "She didn't touch ours."

"Probably because she has excellent taste," Bess said with a mischievous look.

Nancy groaned and tossed a pillow at Bess, who batted it away with her hands. "This is serious. Aren't you the least bit suspicious?" Nancy asked.

"Lighten up, Nan," Bess said. "This is our vacation!" She slipped into the bathroom, calling out, "I've got the first shower!"

An hour later, dressed in shorts, T-shirts, and sneakers, Nancy, Bess, and George were ready to hike into Chora. Armed with their guidebook and instructions from Zoe, the girls set off on the mile-long walk to town.

"Did you guys notice the tension between Zoe and that guy Theo before?" Nancy asked as they trudged uphill on a paved road that crossed the rocky hillside.

Bess nodded. "I got the feeling that Zoe resents him. Maybe they didn't break up on great terms."

"When we were in Olympia, Zoe did mention something about a guy who broke things off," George said. "Theo seems like a nice guy, though."

Bess wiggled her eyebrows suggestively at her cousin. "That's a rave from you," she said. "Do I detect the start of a new romance?"

"No way." George raised her hands defensively. "Kevin's the only guy on my mind these days." George really liked her boyfriend, sports commentator Kevin Davis. Even if there had been a lot of strain between them because

Kevin's job required him to travel frequently, Nancy knew that George was serious about their relationship.

"Well, I think Theo's adorable," Bess said. She giggled and added, "So's Dimitri."

"Face it, Bess," George said. "You're in love with love."

They had just rounded a crest in the road, and Nancy could see Mykonos's distinctive white windmills in the distance. The five round towers seemed to dominate the harbor from their perch on a hill. Below the windmills, dazzling snow white buildings hugged the shoreline.

As the girls continued, the countryside gave way to meandering alleyways lined with cube-shaped houses. Cars were restricted from the cobblestone streets, but the area was busy with tourists, local merchants, and people leading donkeys with food and supplies strapped to their backs.

"Zoe told me that the buildings are white-washed to protect them from the sun," George said as they passed one house.

"She also warned me about the zigzagging streets," Nancy added. They were just passing a narrow, twisting lane. "They were originally designed to foil pirate raiders, so it's easy to get lost if you don't watch where you're going."

"Don't worry," Bess said. "The maze of streets may have confused pirates, but a determined shopper will always find her way."

Following Zoe's directions, the girls turned

down Matoyianni, the main street of town. Shops, cafés, and bakeries stretched out in front of them. The Greek alphabet, so different from English, made it impossible for the girls to read the signs and letters painted on shop windows. But Nancy noticed that the vendors managed to get their messages across by displaying their merchandise.

"Oh, wait a minute," Bess said, stopping in front of a stationery store. "That's the most adorable statue I've ever seen."

Nancy paused to see what had caught Bess's eye. In the window of the small shop sat a tiny white replica of one of Mykonos's windmills. It was surrounded by miniature white houses, fish, boats, and even a pelican. "It is an amazing piece of craftsmanship," she agreed.

"I'll bet the sails even move," Bess said. "I wish I'd cashed some traveler's checks, but I left them in the safe at the hotel. I don't have much Greek currency—just a few drachmas."

"Thank goodness," George said with an exaggerated sigh. "Otherwise, we'd have to hire a donkey to carry your purchases back to the inn."

Nancy and George followed as Bess went into the shop. The small room was jammed with floor-to-ceiling shelves stocked with international newspapers, magazines, postcards, and writing paper. An elderly man with white hair and a wooden pipe clenched between his teeth sat next to a counter against one wall.

When Bess pointed out the windmill to the shopkeeper, he handed it to her so she could have a closer look. "I make," he said, pointing to his chest.

"You did?" Bess said. "Oh, I love it. This is the perfect birthday gift for my mother." Her blue eyes sparkled—until she saw the price. "I guess I'll have to come back after I change more money," she told the elderly shopkeeper.

After thanking him for his help, the girls left the shop. "I wish he hadn't put it back on display," Bess said, pausing outside the shop as the shopkeeper reached down and replaced the statue in the window. "What if someone else buys it?"

"Relax, Bess," Nancy assured her. "Why don't you cash a traveler's check at the hotel? If there's time, we can make a quick trip back here before dinner—"

"The gorgeous American girls!" a familiar voice interrupted Nancy.

Nancy turned and immediately recognized Dimitri, the photographer from the beach. His dark curls glistened in the sunlight.

"That's us!" Bess said, grinning at him.

"Would you like a photo here in Chora?" Dimitri asked, raising his camera.

"No, thanks," Nancy replied. "We were just doing some shopping."

"Ah, in the shop of my good friend Spiros," Dimitri said, nodding at the stationery store. "That is my studio, just above." He pointed to a narrow white stone staircase along the side of the building that led to a room just above the shop.

Bess brightened. "You have your own studio?"

"Of course," Dimitri boasted, never taking his eyes off Bess. "I need a darkroom for my business. I have all the latest equipment."

"I'd love to see the studio," Bess told him. "Could you give us a little tour?"

"Now?" Dimitri hesitated. "I've been very busy today. It's a mess." A group of Japanese tourists caught Dimitri's eye, and he excused himself to snap a few photographs. "I will see you later, I hope," he told Bess.

Nancy was surprised at Dimitri's abrupt switch. One minute the guy was melting over Bess, the next minute he seemed to freeze. Bess had noticed his behavior, too. "I can't decide if he was trying to get a date or give me the brush-off," she said. Shrugging, she added, "Well, I'm not going to let it ruin my day. Come on, guys."

The main street ended at a busy waterfront strip. The crescent-shaped harbor was ringed by hotels, cafés, and tavernas. Small fishing boats skimmed along the water. It all looked tempting. Nancy wasn't quite sure which way to turn first.

Bess persuaded Nancy and George to go into a pastry shop. "After all," she reminded them as they walked inside and peered into a glass case full of cakes and honey pastries, "we won't be eating dinner for a few more hours."

After buying honeyed pastries called *baklava*, the girls turned back up the main street, retracing their steps through the maze of narrow lanes toward the hotel.

"We might as well go straight to the office,"

Bess said when they reached the hotel half an hour later. "I can get my traveler's checks and passport for ID." For security reasons, the hotel requested that all valuables, including passports, be left in the office safe.

The three girls entered the arched double doors of the main building and went to the lobby desk, which was a crescent-shaped cutaway in one of the stucco walls. Zoe was behind the tiled counter, bent over the registration book.

When Bess told her about the miniature she had found in Chora, Zoe smiled and closed the registration book. "You should probably take your passports with you when you leave the hotel grounds," Zoe told them. "But I'll be happy to cash your traveler's checks. Let me get your envelope from the safe." She disappeared through a doorway behind the front desk.

Zoe returned a few minutes later, a grim frown on her face.

"What's the matter?" Nancy asked.

"It's the safe," Zoe told her. "Someone has broken into it!"

21

Chapter

Three

"Oh, no!" Bess cried. She and George exchanged a look of alarm.

"I don't know how it happened," Zoe said. "We always keep that safe locked, but when I went to dial the combination, the door just swung open."

George shot Nancy and Bess a worried look. "Our passports were in there," she pointed out. "And our traveler's checks."

"Has anything been stolen?" Nancy asked.

Zoe's brown eyes were filled with worry. "I don't know. Many things were left behind. Maybe nothing was stolen at all," she said hopefully. "I'll have to check the contents of the safe against our log book." Reaching under the counter, she pulled out a fat notebook and turned to a page with dozens of entries penciled in.

"Looks as if that will take a while," George said. "Do you want us to help?"

"Would you mind?" Zoe asked, looking grateful. "The inventory will go faster that way."

Nancy, Bess, and George joined Zoe behind the check-in counter, then followed her through the doorway and into the back office.

The rosy light of dusk streamed into the room through the slats of a shaded window. On the wall just inside the door was a board with hooks for extra keys to the guest rooms. A metal safe rested on the floor in the far corner, behind a desk covered with stacks of invoices and registration forms.

"First, let me remove everything," Zoe said. She knelt down beside the square gray safe and pulled out a plastic carton containing stacks of manila envelopes. Nancy, Bess, and George gathered around Zoe as she stood and placed the carton on the desk.

"I can't stand the suspense," Bess said, flipping through the envelopes to find the one marked with her name.

"Me, either," George said. She found her envelope and Nancy's and pulled both out.

Checking in her pouch, Nancy was relieved to find her passport and traveler's checks, just as she'd left them. She leafed through the passport, noting the visas stamped on the blue-green pages printed with a bald eagle. "Everything's here," she reported.

"Mine checks out, too," George said.

When Bess said nothing, Nancy looked over at

her. Bess's mouth had fallen open, and there was a look of shock on her face. "My passport's missing!" she said in a horrified whisper.

"Are you sure?" Nancy asked. She leaned over Bess's shoulder as Bess looked into the envelope once again. The traveler's checks were there, Nancy saw, but Bess's passport was gone.

"Maybe it ended up in someone else's envelope," Zoe said hopefully.

George nodded toward the open ledger. "Let's go over the inventory and see."

As Zoe read off the names written in Greek in the inventory ledger, George and Bess checked the contents of each envelope. While they worked, Nancy paced the office, looking for a clue as to who might have tampered with the hotel safe.

Kneeling beside the safe, she looked inside and ran her fingers over the walls of the empty interior. Since there was no damage to the safe, Nancy deduced that either someone knew the combination or was an expert at combination locks. Whoever it was must have been in a hurry, she thought, since they hadn't even closed the safe.

"Who has the combination to the safe?" Nancy asked Zoe.

"Just my father and me," Zoe answered.

"Do you remember who opened the safe last?"

Zoe frowned. "Not really. Things were so hectic today, with that British tour group checking out and a few families checking in. I must have gone into the safe nearly a dozen times myself. But it's not like Papa—or me—to forget and leave it unlocked."

She returned to the inventory with grim determination. "Let's see if anything else is missing," she said.

"A diamond necklace!" Bess remarked as a glittering necklace spilled out of one envelope.

"We've come across a lot of cash, too," George added. "It's hard to believe that a thief would leave all this behind."

Good point, Nancy thought, checking the area around the safe. A shelf of ledgers seemed undisturbed, as did the wooden file cabinet beside the safe. It looked as if whoever had opened the safe and stolen Bess's passport knew exactly where to look for it. And it wouldn't be hard for a staff member to watch Zoe or her father open the safe and remember the combination.

"Who uses this room?" Nancy asked Zoe.

"My father uses it as an office. And sometimes the desk clerks and the cleaning staff come in here," Zoe explained. "They need extra keys from the board when there aren't enough master keys to go around."

Nancy immediately thought of Niki Christofouros. Since she was one of the hotel's maids, no one would question her appearance in the office. And the girls *had* caught her going through Bess's luggage. What if Niki had been trying to steal Bess's passport? Once she saw that it wasn't in the room, maybe she had looked in the hotel safe. The question was, why would she do such a thing?

Nancy decided not to say anything about Niki for the moment. She didn't want to implicate the girl without solid evidence, since Niki could lose her job over this. Just to be safe, though, Nancy suggested that Zoe question the entire hotel staff. In the meantime, Nancy would do some of her own checking on Niki.

"Oh, no! Not another one," Bess groaned a few minutes later. She held up an envelope marked Leo Nelson. "His passport is missing, too," she told Zoe.

George was frowning into another envelope. "Make that three missing passports," she said. "Joseph Seidel's isn't in his envelope."

Zoe circled the two names on her inventory sheet. "Two American men—and Bess," she said wearily.

Luckily, the remaining envelopes contained everything they were supposed to. When the girls were finished, Zoe pushed away the list and leaned back in the desk chair. "So three passports were stolen in all. I can't believe this is happening. It's not good for the hotel. If word gets out, we'll lose customers."

"Not to mention the fact that three passports are now in the hands of strangers," George said.

Bess drew her breath in sharply. "I don't like the idea of someone using my passport illegally," she said in a shaky voice.

"You'll need to get a new one," George advised her.

Leaning over, Zoe squeezed Bess's hand. "I'm so sorry," she said. "The police will know the best way to report it to your embassy."

Just then a tall, husky man with salt-and-pepper hair walked into the room. He assessed the scene, a bewildered expression on his face, then addressed Zoe in rapid-fire Greek. She answered, nodding at Nancy, Bess, and George as she talked.

"This is my father, Kostas Kavalis," Zoe said, introducing the man to Nancy, Bess, and George.

Mr. Kavalis gave each of the girls a hearty handshake. "I'm very sorry about your passport, Bess. I will report it to the police immediately." He glanced back at Zoe's list and frowned. "I must notify those two American men, too."

Shaking his head, Zoe's father went into the front office to call the police.

Nancy sat down on the edge of the desk and mulled over the situation. Three passports had been taken, but dozens of others had been left behind. The thief hadn't touched any of the cash or jewels, either. It didn't make sense.

"What are you thinking, Nan?" George asked.

"Just that the thief seemed to know exactly what he or she was looking for and where to find it. I hope the police can tell us why someone would take three passports and leave everything else."

"I hope so, too," Zoe said. "This is very upsetting."

27

Nancy turned to Zoe. "Please don't be insulted, Zoe, but under the circumstances, I'd feel a lot better if George and I could keep our passports and traveler's checks with us."

"Of course," Zoe said. "I understand perfectly." She went through the envelopes and handed Nancy and George theirs.

When an officer finally arrived, Nancy's questions had to wait until a barrage of Greek questions and answers had flown among Zoe, her father, and the policeman. Zoe introduced the uniformed man as Officer Rossolatos.

At last Officer Rossolatos turned to Bess. He was a heavyset, gray-haired man with a wide, curled mustache. In heavily accented English, he instructed her to report her stolen passport to the U.S. Embassy in Athens. "If you tell them your passport number, there will be no problem to replace it," he said.

"My passport number!" Bess repeated worriedly. "I was supposed to write it down. I *knew* there was something I forgot to do before we left River Heights."

"Why don't you call the embassy now?" Mr. Kavalis offered. "I will help you." He grabbed the carton of guests' valuables. "And these I will put in the safe in our apartment," he added gravely, "where no one else can get to them."

Nancy knew this was her chance to question the officer. "Excuse me, but don't you think it's odd that the thief left with only three passports?" she asked him.

Officer Rossolatos seemed surprised by Nancy's question, until Zoe explained that Nancy was a detective in the United States. "A detective, on our island—we are honored," he said, bowing graciously. He went on to explain, "In the criminal world American passports are prized because they allow access to the United States. They also allow easier passage through Europe."

"So you think Bess's passport will be used by a stranger?" George asked, coming over to stand next to Nancy.

"It is very likely," Officer Rossolatos answered. "They will change the photo, of course. Sometimes they take the booklet apart and replace the entire photo page, inserting a new name and address, too. There are many ways to forge a passport."

Forgery! Nancy's mind reeled at the prospect of Bess's passport in the hands of criminals. What if a crime was committed by someone using Bess's identity? Bess could be in serious trouble. Nancy didn't have much to go on, but she decided to watch out for any clues that might lead her to the trail of the missing passports.

By the time Bess made her call and the police report was complete, it was too late to make another trip back into Chora. The girls decided to take it easy and have a late dinner in the hotel's taverna. Nancy went to get Mick in his room, and soon the teenagers were sitting at a table on a terrace that overlooked the Aegean Sea.

"We just got here, and already you girls are involved in a mystery," Mick said after the girls told him about the passport theft.

"It *is* a mystery," Zoe added. "I spoke to the hotel staff, and no one has any clue as to who might have broken into the safe."

Nancy finished buttering a roll, then turned to Zoe. "Did anyone seem upset by your questions?"

"Not really," Zoe replied. "But one of the maids, Niki Christofouros, seemed nervous when I mentioned Bess's name."

Bess exchanged a curious look with Nancy. "We've met Niki," Nancy said, without mentioning how. She didn't want to get the maid into trouble unless she had more to go on.

"I'm beginning to feel like one of those people in *Casablanca* who can't escape until their papers come," Bess said, stabbing a tomato in her Greek salad. "I must have tried to reach the embassy a dozen times, but I couldn't get through to them."

"Our phone system is unreliable," Zoe told her, "especially during the busy summer season. You'll get through eventually."

Bess tried to smile. "Thanks for cashing my traveler's checks, even though I don't have my passport," she told Zoe. "I hope that miniature windmill won't be sold before tomorrow."

"This store—it contains many tiny replicas—boats and fish and things?"

"That's the one!" Bess said, nodding excitedly.

"It is owned by a man named Spiros. He is a friend of my father's," Zoe continued. "If you like, I will call Spiros and ask him to hold the windmill for you," she offered.

"Would you?" Bess asked. "Tell him I'll stop by as soon as we get back from Delos tomorrow."

Zoe nodded. "It's the least I can do. I hope this theft doesn't ruin your stay here in Mykonos."

George looked over at Bess, who was smiling at a passing waiter. "I don't think there's any chance of that," she said.

Nancy was awakened early Tuesday morning by the sounds of the island coming to life. After throwing back the crisp white sheets, she pushed open the wooden shutters and stepped onto the balcony.

All around her, Mykonos was bustling. Hotel workers wheeled carts of food along the path below her. To her left, three mopeds raced up the hill toward Chora. Motorboats and sailboats zigzagged through the shimmering sea on the horizon, and a group of college guys jogged along the beach.

She was watching the joggers when she spotted a young man and woman standing in the sand at the bottom of the path from the hotel. From their gesturing arms, they seemed to be arguing, though Nancy couldn't hear them from the balcony.

She blinked as she recognized the white uniform and blue apron worn by the maids at the hotel. The girl was Niki, Nancy realized, and she was talking to Dimitri, the photographer.

Curious, Nancy leaned against the balcony rail

and watched. Niki was shaking her head ada-mantly. She reached into a large tote bag, took out a manila envelope, and thrust it into Dimitri's hands. Then she waved Dimitri off, turned away, and stalked up the path to the inn.

What's inside that envelope? Nancy wondered. It was certainly large enough to contain three passports. And considering Niki's suspicious be-havior, Nancy wouldn't be surprised if the maid was the one who had stolen the passports. She still didn't know *why* Niki would steal them, but she was definitely going to try to find out.

"Wake up, you guys," Nancy said, going back into the room. While Bess and George sleepily got out of bed, Nancy told them what she had just seen.

"That definitely seems suspicious," Bess said, pushing her hair back with a headband and going into the bathroom to wash her face.

George glanced at the watch resting on her bedside table. "Too bad we can't do anything about it now. We still have to get dressed and eat breakfast, *and* Bess has to call the embassy in Athens," she said. "We'd better hurry if we're going to catch the boat to Delos at ten-fifteen."

Two hours later Nancy stood beside Mick on the deck of a thirty-foot fishing boat that was used as a ferry in the summer. Tourists milled along the deck, taking in the sunshine and the views. Bess, George, and Zoe stood by the rail, tossing bread crumbs to the gulls that flew along-side the boat, while Nancy and Mick watched.

As Nancy turned toward Mick, he slipped an arm around her shoulders and pulled her close.

"Look at you, with your white sundress and golden tan," he said, "You're beginning to look like an Aussie girl."

"I hope that's good," Nancy said.

"Good? You look fabulous!"

Nancy couldn't help thinking that he looked pretty good himself, in his khaki shorts and white T-shirt.

"We're almost there," Zoe said, joining Nancy and Mick as the boat nosed toward a bare green island that was no more than a few miles long. Already Nancy could see the ruins of a huge, pillared building on a hill above the tiny harbor.

"It doesn't look as busy as Mykonos," Bess observed.

Zoe nodded. "Delos is mostly a museum. Once the tourists leave at the end of the day, it's deserted, except for a small hotel, government guards who protect the ruins—and the lizards who live among the ruins."

"Ugh," Bess groaned. "Lizards?"

"Don't worry—they don't bite," Zoe said with a laugh.

As the boat docked, the teenagers moved toward the ramp where the other passengers were beginning to gather. They waited at the back of the crowd for their chance to disembark. Nancy was just about to step onto the walkway when she noticed the uniformed guards stopping the passengers as they got off the boat.

"What's going on over there?" she asked Zoe.

The Greek girl frowned in confusion. "Those men are from the Delos police," she said. "But they don't usually question tourists. I wish I could hear what they're saying."

"I can," Mick said, wheeling back toward Bess. "They're asking for passports."

George craned her neck to see over the crowd. "It looks as if they're turning one couple away."

The color drained from Bess's face. "Passports? But we're still in Greece. I didn't think I'd need a passport for this."

"I don't understand," Zoe said as the group hesitated at the edge of the gangway. "They usually don't check passports here."

"What am I going to do?" Bess asked worriedly. "That stolen passport is going to ruin the rest of my trip!"

Chapter

Four

NANCY TOOK another look at the two guards. They were wearing khaki uniforms and had stern expressions on their faces. She hoped they were friendlier than they looked.

"Tell them the truth, Bess, that your passport was stolen," Nancy advised, taking Bess by the arm and walking down the ramp with her. "Relax, we won't leave you."

At the end of the gangway the two girls paused before the officers. "Passports?" one officer, a young man, asked curtly.

While Nancy turned her passport over for inspection, Bess began talking rapidly, trying to explain about her stolen passport. The two guards seemed utterly confused until Zoe stepped in and translated, speaking to them in Greek. At last she turned back to Bess.

"They don't want to let you on the island," she said apologetically. "They say they cannot allow a security risk today."

Nancy blinked. Bess, a security risk? She was about to defend her friend when Mick stepped up to the guards and handed over his passport. "I can vouch for this young lady, Officer," he said, clapping a hand on Bess's shoulder.

The young officer was ready to dismiss him, but his partner, an older man, paused and pointed to the diplomat's seal on Mick's passport. Nancy could see that the guards were impressed. In Geneva Nancy had learned that Mick's father was an Australian diplomat. Would the Greek police dare to cross someone with diplomatic ties?

She held her breath as the young officer clapped Mick's passport shut and returned it to him. "You may go," he told Bess in heavily accented English. "But you must contact the American embassy today to get new papers."

"I will—I mean, I already did," Bess said, backing away.

A moment later the rest of the group had passed the guards' inspection. Nancy gave a huge sigh. "That was a close call," she said as they clambered along the dirt landing next to the ramp.

"I wonder why they beefed up security today?" George asked, glancing back at the police officers.

"Good question," Nancy said. For a brief

moment she wondered if there was some link between the security check and Bess's stolen passport. Then she shook herself. Not *everything* that happened in the world was a mystery.

The group paused at the ticket kiosk just a few yards away from the dock, and Zoe helped everyone count out the entrance fee. Then Nancy turned toward the island's ruins.

"Delos was the religious center of ancient Greece," Zoe explained. "Most of the buildings here were built to honor the gods. Huge festivals were held with singers, dancers, processions, horse races, and athletic contests. The island is small, so we can tour it on foot in a few hours."

"Just lead the way," Bess said cheerfully, following Zoe as she took a right turn from the boat landing in the harbor.

Nancy smiled, glad that sightseeing seemed to be taking Bess's mind off the passport problem. Soon after, Nancy, too, was absorbed by the houses they visited, with colorful mosaics and geometrically patterned tiles.

The group worked their way through the many houses that were scattered along the uphill path to Mount Kynthos, the tallest point on the island. Nancy was nearly out of breath by the time she reached the summit. But when she stood overlooking the entire island, she knew it was worth the climb. The mixture of green fields and smooth marble ruins made Delos a land that time forgot.

"You've been awfully quiet," Mick said, coming up to her and placing his hands on her shoulders.

"I guess I've been daydreaming," Nancy said. "Can you imagine what it must have been like to live on this island two thousand years ago?"

"So you're drawn to faraway places, eh? I'd love to show you Australia sometime." Mick stepped around to face Nancy and took her hands in his. "Promise me you'll come visit."

Nancy laughed. "Oh, sure. I'll just jet over when I have a free weekend."

"I'm not kidding," Mick said, his expression serious.

He actually meant it, she realized. "Mick, I'd love to see Australia, but—"

"Don't worry about details," he said, placing a finger over her lips. "We'll work it out."

Nancy was thoughtful as she and Mick followed the others down the hill toward lush palm groves. Soon they arrived at a walkway lined by six grand sculptures of lions stretching toward the east.

"This is called the Terrace of the Lions," Zoe explained.

"It's hard to believe they're two thousand years old," Bess said.

Still thinking of Mick's invitation, Nancy didn't say much as the others commented on the statues. Mick was suddenly quiet, too. He wandered to one of the far lions while George, Zoe, and Bess strolled on, heading back toward the harbor.

Nancy was about to follow when she spotted a photographer with curly black hair poised behind the base of one of the lions. She moved around the lion until she was face to face with Dimitri.

"Yásou," he said, greeting her in Greek as he adjusted a camera tripod. "You are one of the American girls staying in Mykonos, no?"

"That's right," Nancy said, her eyes skimming over Dimitri's bags of equipment. He was using a sophisticated camera with a long lens. "No more pictures of tourists?" Nancy asked him.

"Not today. Today I'm taking beautiful photographs, which I will make into postcards in my studio," he said proudly.

This guy loves to exaggerate, Nancy thought. "Don't you need special equipment to make postcards?" she asked.

"Of course," he agreed. "But my studio is the best on the island of Mykonos. One of the best in all of Greece! It has everything I need."

Including everything you need for forging passports? Nancy wondered, remembering the envelope she had seen Niki hand him on the beach that morning.

"I'd love to see it," she said, watching Dimitri carefully. "In the States I'm an amateur photographer." She was bending the truth, but she thought that Dimitri might believe her.

Instead, he seemed to withdraw. "My equipment is far too technical to interest you."

"I'm a fast learner," Nancy insisted.

"It is not a good idea," Dimitri said, forcing a smile.

Nancy had the distinct impression that there was something in his studio that Dimitri didn't want her to see.

Just then Mick came around the statue and took Nancy's hand. "We'd better get going if we want to catch up with the others," he said.

After saying goodbye to Dimitri, Nancy and Mick continued down the stone-paved path toward the boat landing. During the ride back to Mykonos, she mulled over the encounter with Dimitri. If his studio contained equipment that could make postcards, it had to be fairly sophisticated—maybe sophisticated enough to create a good replica of a passport page.

That thought was still nagging at her when the teens sat down to a late lunch at the hotel's taverna. Zoe had decided to join her father, so Nancy, Mick, George, and Bess shared a table.

"You look as if you're lost in space," George told Nancy as she passed around a platter of *moussaká,* a casserole made of layers of eggplant and ground meat covered in a zesty sauce.

"I've been thinking about Bess's passport and wondering who on this island could pull off a forgery," Nancy said. Lowering her voice, she shared her thoughts about Dimitri's studio. "All that 'special equipment' could come in handy for passport forgeries—especially if he has three American passports to work with."

"Wow," Bess said, stabbing a chunk of juicy eggplant. "Do you think he's the forger?"

40

"It's possible," George said. "Niki had access to the room with the safe, *and* Nancy saw her give something to Dimitri this morning. Maybe she agreed to steal the passports and sell them to him."

Nancy had been thinking the same thing. "I still don't have any proof, though. I really want to check out Dimitri's studio. He was reluctant when I said I wanted to see it . . ."

"So maybe the stolen passports are there," Mick finished for her.

"Would the forger have to be on this island?" George asked. "I mean, maybe the thief took the passports to Athens to have them altered."

"Maybe," Nancy agreed. "But we saw the beefed-up security on Delos today. If security is that tight all over, there's a good chance that the thief—and the passports—are still on Mykonos."

After lunch Bess decided to go to Chora to purchase the windmill from Spiros's shop. Zoe and George had already decided to stay behind and squeeze in a swim before the engagement party that night, but Mick and Nancy opted to go along with Bess.

When they got to the town, the labyrinthine streets were empty except for a few dogs napping in shaded doorways.

"That's right!" Nancy said, slapping her forehead. "Zoe told us yesterday that it's just like in Italy. The businesses close up for siesta from two to five."

41

"Maybe the shop with my windmill is open, though," Bess said hopefully. But when they reached Spiros's shop, the door was locked and the lights were off.

Mick peered through the glass door into the darkness. "What's next?" he asked.

Nancy was beginning to think the trip would be a waste of time. But as her gaze landed on the building's second story, she murmured, "I'd still like to check out Dimitri's studio."

Looking up and down the deserted street, Mick said, "Maybe he hasn't returned from Delos yet." He climbed the narrow white staircase that led to the studio door, then knocked. "And if no one's home, what's the harm in having a quick look?"

When no one answered, Mick looked through the window next to the door. "I don't see anyone," he said. He reached through the open window, stretched, and turned the bolt on the door. "So much for security," he said, and grinned.

He pushed the door open and leaned inside. "The coast is clear, but he could turn up while we're snooping around."

Nancy turned to Bess. "Why don't you stay out here and keep a lookout?"

"Okay." Bess sat in a shady spot at the bottom of the stairs while Nancy joined Mick at the door. "But try to make it quick. I'm roasting."

Inside the studio the first thing Nancy noticed was the wide array of equipment. In the shadowed light she could see a large copy machine, a paper cutter, a light box, an overhead projector, and other equipment. Fake background drops were stacked in one corner.

Although Nancy wasn't an expert, she could see that Dimitri hadn't exaggerated about his studio. "Pretty impressive," she murmured.

From the way Mick whistled through his teeth, she could tell that he agreed. "This color copier is really something," he said, leaning over the huge machine. "This baby can do anything. It can make copies bigger, smaller, darker, lighter— hardly the type of thing you'd expect to find in a vacation resort. I'll bet—"

Mick was interrupted by Bess's loud voice. "Dimitri! Oh, good. I've been waiting for you!"

"Quick!" Mick whispered. "He's coming."

Nancy's eyes darted to the back of the studio, looking for a way out. She saw only a solid, windowless wall. "Mick, there's no back door!" she whispered.

Just then she heard footsteps on the stairs.

Nancy's heart raced as she and Mick dropped to the floor behind the huge copy machine.

They were trapped—and there was no way out!

Chapter

Five

NANCY HUNCHED BEHIND the machine, holding her breath. She could barely make out Bess's voice over the pounding in her own ears.

"It's really important," Bess said persuasively. "It's such a beautiful day—you know, what we call in America a Kodak moment. I just have to capture it on film. Can you take my picture standing next to the fishing boats in the harbor?"

"I'm sure that would be a beautiful photo," Dimitri said, gushing with flattery. "But can we do it later? I've just returned from Delos, and I need to unload—"

"But this camera will be perfect," Bess persisted. "You'll need a good camera to capture the bright sunlight, the deep blue sea . . . and me."

After a moment's pause Dimitri sighed. "For you, I will do it," he said at last.

Way to go, Bess! Nancy thought. She and Mick stayed hidden until they heard the footsteps retreat.

"It's a good thing Dimitri has a thing for Bess," Mick whispered when the coast was clear. "Otherwise, we'd be dead meat right now."

Nancy stood up and brushed off her sundress. "I want to finish checking out this equipment," she told Mick. "We'd better hurry."

She wasn't surprised to see a small darkroom with vats of processing solution. In addition to the color copier, she found a hot-glue gun, a giant stapler used to bind books, and a machine with the word *Artograph* embossed on it.

"I've seen that before in art studios," Mick said, tapping the Artograph. "It's used to project an image on paper or canvas so that the artist can trace over it. With this machine Dimitri could copy just about any design."

Nancy let out a low whistle. "Including anything that might be used for passport paper. Here's a laminating machine, too—and acetate," she added, lifting up a sheet of clear plastic from a shelf along the wall. "This is the stuff they use for that clear plastic coating over a passport photo."

"This studio has a lot more equipment than a simple island photographer would need," Mick said. "Dimitri could definitely be using it to forge passports."

Nancy was searching the row of file cabinets

along one wall. She opened one drawer and pulled out a basket containing thick darning needles and twine. "A sewing basket?" she said, shaking her head as she stuffed it back into the drawer. "I still haven't found anything that directly relates to passports."

"Such as?"

"Printed passport covers or that patterned paper they use for the pages. Even discarded passport photos," Nancy answered.

Mick picked up an envelope from the top of a worktable and looked inside. "This might fit the bill," he said excitedly. "Pictures of a young woman—a rather attractive one, at that."

"What?" Nancy spun around to look at the two sheets of photographic paper he was holding. "Those are contact sheets," Nancy said. "Photographers use them all the time. That way they can look at the negative-size prints and decide what they want to blow up." She looked closer at the square shots of a girl's face. "It's Niki!"

"That maid you were talking about?" Mick asked. "The one who gave Dimitri an envelope?"

Nancy nodded. "She must have handed him *this* envelope. Don't you see, Mick? Dimitri is probably going to slip one of these photos onto Bess's passport so Niki can get into America!"

Nancy and Mick searched the rest of the studio for the stolen passports but came up empty-handed. Besides the photos of Niki, they found a few packets of portraits, but nothing that might be used as a passport photo.

"We still don't have nearly enough evidence to

go to the police," Nancy said, sighing with disappointment. "We'll just have to keep an eye on Dimitri and see if we can catch him in the act."

"We're so lucky to be included in a family party," Bess said as the girls left their room that evening.

"Zoe said that there'll be folk music—and maybe even some plate-throwing," George added.

She led the way to the terraced lawn adjoining the inn's taverna. As they crossed the hotel grounds, Nancy had to admit that it was a perfect night for an engagement party. The wine-dark sea, the lemon-scented air, and the starry sky were a romantic backdrop, perfect for two people who were going to be married.

The party area was festooned with hanging baskets of flowers and flickering candles. A long buffet table was arranged along one side of the dance floor, which had been set on the patio near the taverna. Although Nancy couldn't see them, she could smell the smoke of fire pits on the far side of vine-covered trellises.

"I don't see Zoe," Nancy said, scanning the crowd of guests who were milling about the tables, laughing and talking. She was eager to fill Zoe in on what she and Mick had discovered in Dimitri's studio.

"She must be helping out inside," George guessed.

Nancy didn't see Niki, either, but she hoped the maid was there. She wanted to talk to her as soon as possible about the photos—and Bess's stolen passport.

Nancy, Bess, and George found Mick at a small table, clinking glasses with Theo. Dressed in a copper-colored linen shirt and smart black jeans, Mick looked heartbreakingly handsome.

"Join us!" Theo said, standing up to pull some chairs over for the girls. He was wearing formal black slacks and a white cotton shirt that showed off his tan.

"You look smashing," Mick whispered in Nancy's ear as she sat next to him.

Nancy smoothed the skirt of her royal blue minidress. "Are you trying to get on my good side, Devlin?" she teased, grinning at Mick.

"Who, me?" Mick said innocently.

He waved at a passing waiter and ordered three soft drinks for Nancy, Bess, and George. "Theo was just telling me about Dragonisi, the islet off the coast of Mykonos," Mick told the girls. "He's been spending a lot of time fishing there."

Nancy tried to remember what she had read about Dragonisi in her guidebook. "Isn't that the deserted islet that's riddled with caves?"

"Not to mention a legendary dragon?" Bess added.

Theo laughed. "The dragon hasn't been seen for hundreds of years, but the caves are worth exploring. Dragonisi is isolated—very romantic."

Mick placed his hand over Nancy's. "Just the spot for us, eh, Nancy?"

"Sounds great," she agreed. Turning to Bess

and George, she said, "I know we decided that we wanted to visit Naxos, too. What do you guys think? Want to give Dragonisi a shot?"

"Not me," Bess said, tucking her blond hair behind her ears. "I'm taking the noon flight to Athens tomorrow to get a new passport from the American Embassy, remember? After what happened on Delos, I'm not taking any more chances."

"I'm going with Bess," George added. "But there's no point in all of us springing for airfare back to Athens. We can plan on hitting Naxos on Thursday." Turning to Nancy and Mick, she added, "But you guys might as well go ahead and visit Dragonisi tomorrow."

"Tomorrow it is," Mick said with a wide smile. "Can we hire you to take us there?" he asked Theo.

"Tomorrow?" Theo stared down at the table. "I'm sorry, but I can't do it."

Nancy saw that Theo was suddenly uncomfortable with the conversation, although she didn't know why.

"Well, then, we'll just have to find another boat, since Dragonisi is not to be missed," Mick said. "I'll ask Zoe if she has any suggestions."

"Did I hear my name?" Zoe asked, stopping by their table. She was wearing a strapless dress in a deep shade of scarlet.

Mick explained about their plans for the following day. "And Theo cannot take you?" Zoe asked, narrowing her dark eyes. When he said nothing, Zoe quickly assured Mick that she would make the arrangements for the boat. "We'll pack a lunch for you and Nancy to take along."

"That would be great," Nancy said. Excusing herself, she rose from the table and stepped aside with Zoe. She summarized what had happened that afternoon, then asked, "Do you remember seeing Niki in the office yesterday, when the passports were stolen?"

"Niki?" Zoe thought for a moment, then shook her head. "I don't remember, but it's not something I would notice. My father and I trust our staff." She seemed offended that Nancy suspected a staff member.

"Zoe, time is important," Nancy said, trying to make her understand. "We might be able to recover Bess's passport before it falls into the wrong hands. If Niki's involved, it's important that I talk to her as soon as possible."

Zoe hesitated. "You can't talk to her now," she told Nancy. "Today is Niki's day off. She took the ferry to Tinos, to visit her aunt."

Stifling a sigh of disappointment, Nancy asked, "When will she be back?"

"Tomorrow morning. You can speak with her then," Zoe relented. "I'll arrange it." Then she reached out and squeezed Nancy's hand. "For now, please just try to enjoy the party. All this talk of crime is not good on such a lovely night."

With that, Zoe turned back to the crowd at the table and announced, "Please help yourself to the food. The goat has been roasting for hours, and it's been cooked to perfection."

Bess grinned. "I thought I smelled something delic—" She paused, her blue eyes concerned. "Did you say *goat?*"

"Not your everyday River Heights fare," George said, heading over to the buffet table. "But it does smell great."

As Nancy and the others stood in line for food, the smoke of the charbroiled meat made Nancy's mouth water. In addition to the grilled goat meat, there was chicken stewed in tomato sauce, potatoes, rice, and the classic Greek salad of tomatoes, cucumbers, black olives, onions, and feta cheese. Before long the teenagers were back at their table, their plates heaped with food.

"You know, Theo," George said, dipping a hunk of crusty bread into the olive oil from her salad, "we're relying on you to teach us some authentic Greek dances."

Bess looked over at the dance floor, where a few guests were already moving in time to the soft music. The trio of musicians was made up of a violinist, a clarinetist, and a man who played an instrument that resembled bagpipes. "I'd love to learn, but the steps look awfully complicated."

"It's not so difficult. A good dancer listens to the heart," Theo said, his eyes twinkling. "I am sure you can handle that, Bess."

"I'll give it my best shot," Bess said.

As soon as everyone finished eating, Zoe brought the group over to introduce them to her cousin Helena, and Helena's fiancé, Petros. While Bess and George were talking with the bride-to-be, Nancy stole away for a word with

Zoe's father. She asked if he had heard from the police about Bess's passport, but he didn't have any news.

Finally Nancy joined her friends on the dance floor. For the moment she was at a dead end. She decided that she might as well take Zoe's advice and have a good time.

Zoe was walking the group through the steps of the *Stae Tria,* one of the most popular Greek dances. With their hands on one another's shoulders, all the dancers formed a wide circle. The band was playing a slow song, so it was easier to follow along at first.

"You're doing well," Zoe said as George kicked at the air.

"One, two, three, kick, kick," Bess counted aloud, laughing when she missed a step.

Nancy counted along, trying to get the hang of the dance. She couldn't help laughing, too. The lively beat of the music filled the air until almost all the guests joined the circle. Theo added some dramatic effects, leaping through the air and slapping his feet on the floor.

Gradually Nancy fell into the rhythm of the dance. The complicated steps seemed more and more natural as Mick cheered her on. To her amazement, one man danced among the crowd with a bottle balanced on his head. Two other men danced around with dinner plates, which they smashed against a wall with bravado. The song ended, and applause and cheers erupted from the crowd.

"The plate-breaking is a Greek custom called

spasimo," Zoe explained. "We try to keep it at a minimum, or else we'll run out of dishes!"

"I'll bet," Nancy said, laughing.

The dancers were applauding the band when Nancy noticed a sudden movement in the shadows beyond the trellis at the edge of the lawn. She squinted into the darkness, and suddenly she saw a figure.

"Is something wrong?" Mick asked, noticing the expression on her face.

But before Nancy could answer, the stranger stepped out of the shadows. He was tall, with wavy brown hair and a muscular physique. Moving onto the candlelit dance floor, he tapped George on the shoulder.

George spun around, and her mouth fell open. "Kevin!"

Chapter

Six

NANCY COULD HARDLY believe it. It was Kevin Davis, George's boyfriend!

Without a second thought George flung herself into Kevin's arms. He held her close for a tender kiss, then whirled her around. "I'm glad you remember me," he teased.

"What are you doing here?" George asked breathlessly. "I thought you were on assignment."

"I am. I have to meet up with my TV crew on Sunday in Madrid. Until then, I'm all yours—aside from a quick interview I need to do in Athens."

"Terrific!" George stood aside as the others rushed over to say hello to Kevin. No sooner had he been introduced to Mick, Theo, and Zoe than the band launched into a slow, romantic ballad. Within seconds Nancy found herself swept into Mick's strong arms.

"This is called the *ballo,*" she heard Theo say to Bess. "It's a couple's dance, played in honor of the engaged pair."

Bess sighed. "How romantic!"

Turning her head, Nancy saw a starry look in George's eyes as she moved into Kevin's arms. Behind them, Helena and Petros swirled in the center of the dance floor.

When Mick led Nancy over to the edge of the dance floor, she could hear the sea in the distance, lapping against the shore. "It's such a beautiful night," she said, tilting her head back so that she could see the stars glittering in the ink black sky. "I hate for it to end."

"Who says it has to?" Mick pulled her closer, and Nancy smiled, forgetting about Bess's stolen passport. All she could think about was Mick and the delicious feeling of dancing in his arms.

"I know it was my idea to come into town before the flight to Athens," Bess told Nancy the next morning, "but after all that dancing last night, I should have stayed in bed."

Nancy's only response was a yawn. It was almost nine o'clock, but the engagement party had ended very late, and she was a little tired. She and Bess had already rushed through a breakfast of milk and cheese pies in a bakeshop, called a *zacharoplasteion.* Now bleary-eyed, they were walking along the main street of Chora, dodging tourists and donkeys laden with baskets.

George had met Kevin for a morning jog on the beach, and Mick was probably still asleep. Lucky guy, Nancy thought. Since Bess and George were taking a noon flight to Athens, Bess had persuaded Nancy to join her for an early trip into town.

"After all this, I hope my mother likes the statue," Bess said. "Oh—there's the store."

She breathed a sigh of relief when she saw that the stationery store was open. It didn't take her long to pay for the windmill, which Spiros, the owner, had set aside for her after Zoe called him. The silver-haired man chewed on his unlit pipe as he wrapped the windmill in tissue and placed it in a box. He had just offered to gift wrap the box when the phone rang in the back room.

"Please," he said. "Excuse, one moment."

While he was gone, Nancy browsed around the shop. She looked up as the shop door opened and Dimitri stepped in. "It's your friend, the paparazzo," Nancy said under her breath to Bess.

Dimitri lowered a camera case to the floor, then walked behind the counter. "Ah, it is my favorite American girl," he said, winking at Bess. "I will have those photos for you this afternoon. Where is my friend, Spiros?"

"He's in the back," Bess said. "He was just about to wrap that for me"—she leaned over the counter to point to a box—"when the phone rang."

"Ah, then let me take care of it. Spiros and I help each other all the time. We are very good friends." After placing the box on the counter, Dimitri began to search the shelves. "Wrapping paper," he mumbled, pulling out boxes of sealed stationery, cardboard, and notepads—everything *but* wrapping paper.

Nancy was beginning to think Bess would miss her flight to Athens when Dimitri held up a sheet of pale blue paper. "Ah, here we go," he said. "Beautiful paper. But then, my friend Spiros truly appreciates fine craftsmanship."

With a few quick folds Dimitri wrapped the box.

"Thanks—*evcharistó*," Bess said, dropping the package into her tote bag.

"You're welcome," Dimitri said. Just then Spiros returned, and the two men spoke briskly in Greek. Nancy sensed that Dimitri was a little nervous around the older man, though she couldn't imagine why. As Spiros sat down on a stool, Dimitri quickly darted out from behind the counter and picked up his camera case.

"How about a photo of Nancy Drew, the American detective?" he suggested.

Nancy's mouth dropped open in surprise. How did Dimitri know she was a detective? "No, thanks," she told him. "Besides, I'm on vacation."

"But you are famous," Dimitri insisted. "My friend Officer Rossolatos sings your praises."

So that's how he knows, Nancy thought. Did

that also mean Dimitri knew about the passport thefts?

"I don't know about that. . . ." she hedged, looking him in the eye. Was he testing her? She wasn't sure if his naive enthusiasm was real or just a cover-up for a cunning master of forgery. As she and Bess said goodbye and left the store, Nancy resolved to find out.

The two girls were nearly a block away when Bess said, "Dimitri seems to be 'good friends' with everyone on Mykonos."

"It *is* a small island," Nancy said. "Still, I wish he hadn't heard that I'm a detective. It's going to make it harder to pin him down if he's the passport forger."

When Nancy and Bess arrived at the hotel, they found George, Kevin, and Mick lounging in the garden terrace overlooking the sea. George's short brown curls were still damp from her shower, and she was wearing a denim skirt and red, short-sleeved top.

"Ready for our trip?" George asked Bess.

Bess nodded, pulling the wrapped windmill from her tote bag. "Yup. I just want to put this up in our room."

"Have a seat, Nancy," Mick said. He patted an empty chair. "We'll get you some lemonade."

"No, thanks," Nancy told him. "I'm going up to the room with Bess to change. And I'm going to need some sunscreen and a hat if we're going to spend the afternoon on Dragonisi. We'll meet you back here in fifteen minutes, okay?"

When Nancy reached the top of the white

staircase leading to their room, she found that the door was ajar—again! "That's strange," she said, turning back to Bess. Cautiously she pushed on the door and peered inside.

The sight before her made Nancy do a double-take. From the back the young girl in their room resembled Bess. She had on Bess's red straw hat and a matching red bolero jacket. But looking closely, Nancy recognized the skirt and apron of the hotel's housekeeping staff.

It was Niki Christofouros—dressed in Bess's clothes!

Chapter

Seven

Niki," Nancy said, stepping into the room. "What are you doing?"

The dark-haired maid spun around and gasped. "I—" she stuttered, fingering the hem of the red jacket. "Um, Zoe told me you wanted to see me."

"Hey, that's my outfit," Bess observed, more confused than angry.

"I was just—putting it away," Niki said, quickly peeling off the jacket.

This time Bess didn't let Niki off the hook. "Wait a minute," she said, standing with her hands on her hips. "I know you went through my stuff before, and that same day my passport was stolen."

Looking squarely at the maid, Nancy added, "Did you take those passports from the safe?"

"No!" Niki insisted, her brown eyes wide. She shook her head vehemently. "I swear it. I admit I have been looking at your things. But I never stole anything."

"I saw you on the beach yesterday morning—with Dimitri," Nancy said.

Confusion darkened Niki's eyes. "Dimitri?"

Nancy nodded. "I saw you hand him an envelope. Did you give him the passports?"

"No!" Niki insisted. "I gave him back the photographs that he took of me because they were awful! I wanted some photographs of myself to send to—" She paused, searching for the right words. "Agencies in the United States, for being a model. My sister tells me I could be famous. But Dimitri made me look . . . plain, like an ordinary person."

"You wanted pictures for a portfolio?" Bess asked, catching on.

Niki nodded. "I need a port—a portfolio to be a model in America. That is why I was studying those." She pointed to the dresser, where some of Bess's fashion magazines were open. "But I did not take anything."

Nancy looked down at the glossy photos of smiling models. "I don't understand," she said. "Fashion magazines are available here. I've seen them in shops."

"But they are *European* magazines," Niki explained. "I am interested in what is going on in *America*. My sister lives there, and I am going to join her as soon as I have saved enough money."

Bess and Nancy exchanged a look. Nancy could tell that Bess believed Niki's story. She had to admit, the young girl was convincing.

"If it'll help your career, why don't you take these," Bess said, gathering the magazines and handing them to Niki. "I'm sure you'll find some new styles that will look great on you."

"Evcharistô," Niki said, hugging the magazines to her chest. She started toward the door, then turned back when she realized she was still wearing Bess's hat. "I almost forgot," she murmured, smiling. "You have such beautiful clothes." Quickly she put down the hat, picked up her bucket of cleaning supplies, then ducked out the door.

"A fashion ally!" Bess said, clapping her hands together.

Nancy didn't say anything right away. After tossing her penlight, sunscreen, and an orange hat into a canvas bag, she looked at Bess and said, "I still want to check out the stuff about her sister."

"Oh, come on, Nancy," Bess protested, taking the wrapped package out of her tote bag and placing it on the dresser. "What do your instincts tell you?"

Nancy thought for a moment. "That Niki's just a nice girl who wants to be a model. And she had the bad luck to get caught snooping around in your things."

"So you *do* understand," Bess said, grinning. "She's just a slave to fashion—like me."

* * *

Bess and George were in high spirits as they jumped into a cab with Kevin and headed off toward the airport. Kevin had been able to schedule his interview for that afternoon so that the three of them could travel together.

When Nancy met Mick on the terrace after seeing off her friends, her heart did a little leap. He was dressed in black swim trunks and a green T-shirt that hugged his broad, muscular shoulders. "Ready to slay the dragon?" he asked, spinning his baseball cap around on one finger.

"They say the dragon dried up years ago," Nancy told him.

He tapped her nose gently. "Well, if anyone can find the beast, it's ace detective Nancy Drew."

"I'm game," Nancy said, laughing. "But first I have a few things to straighten out with Zoe."

They found Zoe in the hotel's kitchen, supervising the lunch preparations. When Nancy told her about her conversation with the maid, Zoe confirmed that Niki's sister had recently moved to America. "She used to work right here, in our kitchen."

Zoe frowned, thinking over the situation. "I didn't know about Niki's desire to be a model, but I know she has been planning a trip to America. In fact, she asked my father to keep her passport in the family vault so that she wouldn't misplace it."

"Niki already has a passport?" Nancy asked. If

63

Niki was free to travel to the U.S., why would she steal Bess's passport for her own use?

"Yes," Zoe replied. "I should have thought of that last night when you asked about her at the party."

That just about clears Niki, Nancy thought. But she still wanted to pay close attention to Dimitri.

"What a feast!" Nancy exclaimed as she caught sight of the picnic basket that Zoe had prepared for Mick and her.

"Grapes, oranges, cheese, stuffed grape leaves, and pastries," Mick said, popping a grape into his mouth. "This is great, Zoe. Thanks."

A middle-aged man appeared at the kitchen door with his pale blue cap in his hand. He said something in Greek to Zoe, who then turned to Mick and Nancy. She introduced the balding, heavyset man as Nikos, the guide she had hired to take them to Dragonisi.

Soon they were off. Nikos didn't speak much English, Nancy discovered, but she was so wrapped up in the beautiful day that it really didn't matter. She leaned contentedly against Mick as they cruised along, the boat cutting through the water with ease.

Nancy's first glimpse of Dragonisi was of a wild, isolated mass of rock and sand. Nikos circled the island so that she and Mick could get their bearings. One end of the oblong island seemed to be the hot spot for snorkeling. Half a dozen boats were anchored offshore, and Nancy saw three different groups of swimmers who seemed to be taking instruction.

"Hey, check that out!" Mick said, pointing to one of the boats bobbing in the water near the beach. "Isn't that the *Sea Star?*"

Squinting over the sparkling reflection of sunlight on the water, Nancy was able to make out the distinctive star on the boat's yellow hull. "That's it," she said, scanning the beach. "And there's Theo."

No sooner had Nancy spotted him than she saw Theo bounding over to a petite girl with short red hair.

"That's strange," Mick said as their boat coursed ahead. "When I asked him to bring us to Dragonisi he turned me down—and yet, there he is."

Nancy was wondering the same thing as she tied her reddish blond hair into a ponytail and tucked it under her orange baseball cap. "Maybe another group hired him to bring them here," she said.

After circling Dragonisi, Nancy and Mick asked Nikos to drop them off in a secluded area. They chose a rocky beach on the opposite side of the islet from the groups of divers and made arrangements with Nikos to pick them up at the same spot at four o'clock.

Knowing that they would have to wade ashore, Nancy had worn a swimsuit under her clothes. Now she stuffed her shorts, T-shirt, and sneakers into her tote bag. Holding the tote bag over her head, she lowered herself into the water and waded to the beach. Mick followed, balancing his clothes and the picnic basket. Standing on the uneven stretch of sand broken by craggy rock formations, they waved to Nikos as he sped off.

"I don't know about you," Mick said after they found a cozy spot in the shade of a twisted olive tree, "but after that boat ride, I'm starved."

Nancy glanced at the dark cave openings in the rocky hills. "I guess the caves can wait until after lunch," she said.

She opened the picnic basket, and they split up the generous portions of fruit and spread the cheese on the crusty bread. While they ate, they discussed the fading trail of the missing passports.

"I think you're right to keep an eye on Dimitri," Mick said. "He's suspicious, all right."

Nancy sighed. "And he's our only lead, unfortunately. I wish I had more to go on."

"This morning I contacted some friends of my father's at the Australian Embassy in Athens," Mick told her, licking his fingers after eating a stuffed grape leaf. "They'll let me know if they hear of similar thefts—or if they come across any information on Bess's passport."

Half an hour later Nancy was sure she couldn't eat another thing.

"Some more grapes?" Mick offered.

"No, thanks." She was already on her feet and slipping her clothes on over her swimsuit, which had dried in the sun. "I'm dying to explore some of those caves that Theo told us about. This should help light the way," she said, pulling her penlight out of her tote bag.

"That tiny thing?" Mick teased. He reached into the picnic basket and pulled out a high-powered flashlight. "Zoe left this for us," he said, pushing his cap back on his head. "When it comes to caves, you don't want to be left in the dark."

The first cave they explored had an arched opening with a vaulted rock ceiling high overhead. "It's like a Gothic cathedral," Nancy said. A moment later, she laughed as her voice bounced back in an eerie echo.

Inside, they climbed between two huge boulders and found themselves on a narrow path leading into the darkness. "We'd better keep close to each other," Mick said, turning back to take Nancy's hand before he continued. Nancy stepped carefully, watching the beam of Mick's flashlight bounce along the walls ahead.

She nearly ran smack into Mick when he stopped abruptly. "Whoa!" he said, grabbing Nancy by the waist and taking a step back.

"What is it?" she asked. Her eyes followed the beam of light as it moved over the ground in front of them, then dropped off into blackness.

"The path ends—very suddenly," Mick said, dropping to his knees and shining the light down into the pit. "That must be at least a twenty-foot drop, and there's water at the bottom."

Staring into the black hole, Nancy felt her stomach drop. "That was a close call," she said.

They backed away and retraced their steps to the cave entrance. Nancy didn't realize how cool the cave was until she stepped out into the bright sunlight. She rubbed her arms and asked brightly, "What next?"

"You're always ready for the next adventure," Mick said, shaking his head. "That's what I like about you, Nancy. Never a dull moment."

"Come on, Devlin. Don't tell me you're ready to give up after one cave?" Nancy teased.

"Oh, not me. But with your curiosity, you'd go wild in Australia. Just think of it, Nan. A whole continent to explore."

"Sounds great." Nancy had to admit that the idea of visiting the distant continent appealed to her—especially with Mick to show her around. Things were definitely getting serious between them. She was beginning to think that everything back home—her friends, her work, and even Ned—would never be the same for her again, now that she'd met Mick. "Who knows?" she added. "Maybe we'll have a chance to see Australia together."

"You're softening. That's a good sign," Mick said. He leaned close to press a gentle kiss against her lips. "So . . . which cave do you want to tackle next?"

Tugging on her fluorescent orange cap, Nancy surveyed the situation. She could see the openings to three other caves. One was so high that she knew it was out of their reach. Another opening was so narrow that she and Mick would have to crawl through it. She pointed to a square passage that started at the top of a flat, rocky rise. "Let's try that one."

Stepping through the wide mouth of the cave, Nancy and Mick found that the walls narrowed into a dark tunnel. It twisted right, then left, and then they saw a faint haze of light. Nancy was surprised to find that the tunnel ended at an airy chamber, lit by pale sunlight filtering in through an opening in the rock high above.

"It's like a great hall," she said, gazing around the huge space. At the far end of the chamber a pond of dark water, smooth as glass, stretched to the rough stone wall.

"We're not the first people here," Mick commented, switching off the flashlight.

Nancy followed his gaze to a recessed area on their right, where three knapsacks were propped against a boulder. Two sleeping bags were rolled out next to a few orange cushions marked with a star and some Greek letters. Nancy walked over to the boulder, knelt to pick up one cushion, and studied the markings. The first three letters were distinctively Greek, but the last four resembled the English letters *aooa*.

Standing up, she spotted a hearth and cooking utensils just beyond some boulders. "Someone's camping here," she observed. "Maybe we should head back. I feel like I'm intruding on their home." She backed away and accidentally knocked over a lantern.

Leaning down to pick it up, she noticed an envelope on the ground beside it. The flap was partially open, and Nancy glimpsed the edge of a photograph. She looked more closely—and gasped.

"Passport photos?" She looked over the headshots of a dark-haired man. He seemed to have a scar on his face, but the photos were a little blurred, so she couldn't be sure. "Check this out," she said, turning to Mick.

"No time for that," Mick said urgently. "We have to get out of here—and fast."

Hearing alarm in his voice, Nancy dropped the envelope and joined Mick. He was standing next to a stack of wooden cartons. She squinted in the dim light to read the word painted on each of the cartons: Explosives.

"Explosives?" Nancy's heart started pounding. "In here?"

Mick nodded, stepping away from the four cartons. "Enough to blow this place out of the Aegean."

"It's definitely time to go," Nancy said.

She turned abruptly toward the cave's opening, then froze as a man's voice called loudly from the tunnel beyond the cave opening: "Shara! Shara!" He was answered by a woman, who spoke brusquely.

Nancy felt the hair on the back of her neck stand up. The campers were returning—and she had a hunch they weren't going to be happy that she and Mick had discovered their collection of fireworks.

Mick's eyes darted about the chamber. "Looks as if the way we came in is the only way out."

"Not good," Nancy whispered, her nerves twanging. "Mick, if those are the people who own these explosives, they might blow us away!"

Chapter

Eight

NANCY TENSED as the man's voice called again, "Shara!" His voice echoed against the cave walls, so it was hard to tell how far away he was.

"Do you know what he's saying?" she whispered to Mick.

"It's Greek to me," Mick said.

In the tension of the moment Nancy couldn't appreciate his joke. She shivered as she looked frantically around the cold, damp cave for somewhere to hide.

Mick had moved away from the explosives and was running his hands along the rock wall near the passageway to the tunnel. "See that ledge up there, over the opening to the tunnel?" he asked.

Nancy nodded, spotting the ledge that ran over

the doorway, about ten feet from the ground. "But it doesn't lead anywhere."

"We can hide up there—if we can find a way to climb up."

In a flash Nancy was beside him, searching the rock wall for cracks and crevices that they could use as handholds. The voices of the people were getting louder, but still Nancy and Mick hadn't found a break in the rock.

"Quick, give me a boost," Nancy said breathlessly. Mick laced his fingers together so that she could step up from his hands. Desperately she scraped at the rock wall overhead until she felt a triangular wedge she could wrap her fingers around. A moment later she pulled herself up onto the ledge.

Moving fast, she scrambled around, locked her foot into a crevice, and stretched out so that she could help Mick up. Her muscles strained and her body flattened against the rock ledge as Mick grasped her hand and hoisted himself up within reach of the ledge. He had to make it up before they were discovered!

With his free hand Mick grabbed on to the same triangular wedge Nancy had used, and he pulled himself up. He huddled beside her, his face grimy with sweat and dust.

And not a moment too soon. Suddenly the voices were loud and clear, and Nancy knew that the strangers had reached this end of the tunnel. She sank back against the wall as two figures, a man and a woman, entered the rocky chamber below her.

In the pale light that filtered in from the opening above, Nancy could see a short, brawny man with jet black hair and a nasty red scar that stretched from his chin to his ear on the right side of his face. He was wearing shorts, which were sopping wet. Seeing his muscled arms and chest, Nancy knew that he would be a formidable opponent.

The woman was wearing a black one-piece swimsuit. Small-boned and petite, she had short red hair that was slicked back with water. Her features were plain, though something about her seemed familiar to Nancy. Since she was also wet, Nancy guessed that they had just been swimming.

The couple appeared to be arguing as they pulled clothes out of two of the knapsacks. Nancy wondered if the owner of the third knapsack was nearby.

Although she couldn't understand anything the couple was saying, Nancy noticed that the man kept repeating "shara." She made a mental note to ask Zoe if she knew the word. Her ear for languages told Nancy that these people weren't speaking Greek. The rhythm and tone of the language was different from the conversations she had heard at the hotel and in Chora.

A glance at Mick told Nancy that he was studying the couple just as closely as she was. What are we going to do? she wondered. If the couple moved toward the back of the cave, she and Mick might have a chance to slip out through the tunnel without being noticed. But it wouldn't be that easy.

The red-haired woman pulled a towel from her knapsack and marched toward the tunnel. Unfortunately, the man didn't seem inclined to follow her. Resigned to settling in, Nancy shifted her legs.

Suddenly she felt herself sliding. Panic cut through her like a sharp knife. Pebbles and dirt scattered to the ground as Nancy grappled to keep her balance. But it was too late. Alerted by the falling pebbles, the woman looked up—right at Nancy and Mick.

Gritting her teeth, Nancy dropped to the ground. She landed just a few feet from the surprised woman. Any hope of a friendly reception was immediately dashed when the woman assumed a fighting stance. With a fierce cry she squared off and aimed a karate chop right at Nancy's face!

Thinking fast, Nancy dodged the blow, wheeled, and landed a kick to the woman's chest, knocking her to the ground.

The man was scrambling near the knapsack, probably looking for a weapon, Nancy thought.

Before he could act, Mick leapt to the ground beside Nancy. "Out we go!" he shouted, pulling her toward the tunnel. Not daring to look back, Mick and Nancy raced through the narrow passageway as quickly as they could.

When they reached the cave's entrance, Nancy turned away from the flat, sandy beach and darted behind a jagged boulder lodged in the sand.

"Are they following us?" she whispered breathlessly to Mick.

"They will," he answered, "but I think we've got a good lead." He nodded toward a rocky incline that formed a point on the south end of the beach. "We'll have to climb up that hill and hide behind boulders. It's our only chance of losing them."

Without hesitating, they tore off and scrambled up the hill. Glancing back, Nancy saw that Mick was right: The man and woman had chased them onto the beach. She darted behind a boulder, but not before she spotted the glint of a knife in the man's hand.

Nancy's stomach churned as the weight of the situation hit her. These people were armed and dangerous!

Fortunately, she and Mick had enough of a lead to give them an advantage. After a few minutes they managed to lose their pursuers in the rambling, twisted rocks.

As she and Mick continued to put distance between them and the cave, Nancy's mind raced. They had left the picnic basket and her tote bag under the olive tree on the beach, and she knew it wouldn't be safe to return there. Luckily nothing in the bag would help the man and woman track her down.

On the other hand, now she and Mick wouldn't be able to hook up with Nikos, either, and he was their only way home. Unless they could flag down a boat of snorkelers, she and Mick would be stuck on Dragonisi, at least for the night.

Nancy was mulling over the situation when she and Mick reached a low cliff overlooking the water. The sea was a short drop, maybe fifteen feet below them. Nancy sat down to rest. Looking out over the water, she noticed a boat on the horizon, speeding along the islet's shoreline.

"That boat's heading our way. Think we can hitch a ride?" she asked, grabbing Mick's arm.

He shrugged. "It's worth a try."

Nancy took off her bright orange cap and tried to flag down the boat. She was waving frantically when she recognized the boat's yellow hull and distinctive star. It was the *Sea Star*. "Theo!" she shouted.

"Well, fancy that," Mick said. He stood up as the boat swerved toward them and slowed down.

Theo seemed surprised to see Nancy and Mick stranded on the low cliff. Within minutes he had taxied ashore on an inflated dinghy and brought them aboard the *Sea Star*. When Nancy and Mick warned Theo that they were in danger, he sped away immediately, without asking questions.

Nancy waited until the boat was a safe distance from Dragonisi before she filled him in on their close brush in the cave.

"That is amazing!" Theo exclaimed, the wind rippling his hair. "Those caves you were exploring have drop-offs and hidden passages. Did you notice a pond in one of the caves?"

Nancy nodded. "Yes, in the cave that the people were camped in."

"That's called Kea Lake. It has a channel that leads out of the cave—a tunnel of water. It connects to a small pond on the other side of the point, where you flagged me down."

"Do you mean we could have swum out of the cave?" Mick asked, somewhat surprised.

"It is possible," Theo said. "But it is very tricky if you do not know the cave."

"You seem to know Dragonisi well," Nancy told Theo.

He shrugged. "I have maps, but the caves are dangerous. I'm glad you weren't hurt."

"Lucky for us you were in the area," said Mick. "We saw your boat on the other side of the island before lunch. How was the fishing?"

Theo glanced away. "Not so good. No fish today."

Nancy looked over at the empty fishing net and wondered what Theo had been doing all day. "Maybe you saw the people we had the run-in with," she said. "I think they were out swimming before they returned to the cave." She went on to describe the man and woman.

Theo frowned and suddenly became preoccupied with navigating his boat. He definitely seemed uncomfortable with her questions. In fact, she was sure he was hiding something. "I didn't see them," he said, concentrating on the open sea.

Changing the subject, he said, "It will be almost an hour until we reach Chora. In the meantime, I will try to radio Nikos so he does not search for you. Why don't you relax?" he said, nodding toward the seats on the aft deck.

With a sigh, Mick sank onto an orange cushion. "I'm glad that's over."

"We'll have to report it to the police on Mykonos," Nancy reminded him as she sat down next to him. In the frenzy of their confrontation in the cave, she hadn't had time to tell him about the passport photos she found there.

"Wow!" Mick exclaimed once she told him. His green eyes flickered with interest. "Along with the explosives, it all adds up to something illegal—and deadly."

"Do you think those people in the cave are connected to the three passports?"

Mick shrugged. "How do you figure that?"

"I don't know," Nancy said, hugging a cushion to her chest. "But I thought of it when I saw those photos in the cave."

As she spoke, Nancy looked down at the cushion in her arms. Something about it struck a familiar chord in her mind. The square cushion was covered with smooth orange canvas cloth. She turned it over and found that a star and a few Greek letters had been marked on the cushion with a black felt-tip pen. The Greek word ended with the letters *aooa*.

Nancy's eyes widened in surprise. The same cushions had been sitting near the sleeping bags in the cave with the explosives!

Chapter
Nine

W HAT'S WRONG?" Mick asked.

Nancy glanced ahead to make sure that Theo couldn't hear them. Then she showed Mick the marking on the cushion. "I saw the same cushions in that cave."

"Are you sure?" Mick questioned. "We don't know the Greek alphabet. Maybe some of the letters just look the same."

"I'm positive," she said emphatically. "It was a star, followed by these symbols." A quick search of the other cushions on the aft deck revealed that they were all marked the same way.

Mick's eyes darkened, and he said, "Now that I think of it, what was Theo doing on that deserted part of Dragonisi—after he refused to take us there? He could have been on his way to see the people in the cave!"

Nancy tensed. "And remember that woman we saw him talking to, next to the snorkelers? She had red hair . . ."

"Just like the woman in the cave," Mick finished. "I think it's time Theo gave us some solid answers," he added, suddenly on his feet.

Nancy grabbed his arm and pulled him back. "If he *is* involved with those people, we can't afford to confront him while we're out on the open sea."

"Good point." Mick took her hand and settled in for the ride.

Nearly an hour later, as they arrived in Mykonos's harbor, Nancy held up one of the cushions and said to Theo, "These are nice. But what do those letters say?"

"Those are the markings of the *Sea Star*," Theo replied. He threw a line around a wooden stanchion in the marina, then turned to Nancy and traced the handwritten symbols on the cushion. "The name is also marked on the hull of my boat."

"Do any of the other boats have the same cushions?" Nancy asked him.

"Oh, sure. But not with these markings—at least, they shouldn't," Theo said sternly. "I noticed that some of my cushions disappeared a few days ago." He lowered his voice. "But I think some of the older fishermen here at the marina are playing a joke on me."

Mick and Nancy exchanged a look that said they both doubted the story. Mick started to say something, but Nancy shook her head, stopping him.

It wouldn't be wise to press Theo. There were too many questions—about the cushions, about the redheaded woman, about Theo's presence at Dragonisi, and about the deadly explosives. She needed to investigate on her own before she let Theo know how much she suspected.

The hot sun and excitement had taken its toll on Nancy's energy, but she wanted to report the incident on Dragonisi right away. Fortunately, there was a police station located on Mykonos's harbor between a café and a souvenir shop. Inside, Nancy and Mick waited on a bench in a dusty gray room while the desk officer located someone who spoke English.

Finally Officer Rossolatos appeared, with a younger police officer who had short black hair. Nancy and Mick reported the incident on Dragonisi without too much trouble. The only problem was, every time they said something, Officer Rossolatos translated it, and a barrage of conversation—all in Greek—followed. Nancy was dying to know what the men were saying.

She kept hearing one word crop up. It sounded like *"diafevgo."* But when she asked what they were discussing, Officer Rossolatos brushed her questions aside.

"We will send a boat to Dragonisi to look for these people, but please, stay away from that place," he warned Nancy and Mick. "These people . . . they may be very dangerous."

"I'm a world traveler once again!" Bess said, waving her new passport in the air as she pulled out a chair and sat down at the table.

George and Kevin sat down next to her. "Now at least you don't have to worry if anyone asks for ID when we go to Naxos tomorrow."

"Great," said Nancy. She, Mick, and Zoe were already sipping iced fruit drinks at Kounela, a waterside taverna in Chora. They had left a message at the hotel telling Bess, George, and Kevin where to meet them for dinner.

As soon as everyone settled in, the group agreed to let Zoe order up some traditional Greek dishes that they could all share. Then Nancy got a full report on her friends' trip to Athens.

"The passport stuff took a couple of hours," Bess said, taking a sliced orange from the rim of her glass. "Then we got to watch Kevin interview Angelique Seferis! She's just as beautiful as she looks on TV—and nice, too."

"I'm glad you girls could come along," said Kevin. "It made the interview a lot more like fun."

George smiled at him, but Nancy could see that she wasn't as ecstatic as Bess. "Watching you in front of the camera reminded me how hard you work," George told Kevin. "And you're off to Spain on another assignment in a few days."

Kevin placed his hand over George's and gave

it a squeeze. Nancy felt a little sorry for George. It had to be frustrating to be in love with someone who was always on the road.

"Everyone set for Naxos tomorrow?" Bess asked, putting aside her menu.

The group gave a chorus of approval. "The hydrofoil is the fastest way to go," Zoe said. "It will give us more time to explore the island."

Just then a procession of waiters appeared, each bearing a platter of food that made Nancy's mouth water. Zoe explained all the dishes, from cubes of roasted lamb, called *souvlákia,* to spicy meatballs called *ghiuvarlakia.* There were also platters of dried octopus, fish steeped in olive oil, and grape leaves stuffed with spiced meat.

The platters were being passed around the table when Bess inquired, "How was Dragonisi?"

"Poor Nancy and Mick had a terrible time!" Zoe said, stabbing a grape leaf with her fork.

"What happened, Nan?" George asked, a concerned look in her brown eyes.

Nancy and Mick took turns telling the others about their day. First, Nancy recounted the story of their close call in the cave and of finding the explosives and passport photos. "Hardly standard camping gear," she remarked dryly.

"It's an odd coincidence," Kevin said. "But how could they be connected to the passports that were stolen from the hotel?"

Nancy let out her breath in a long sigh. "I'm not sure," she admitted, "but these people are definitely trouble. Maybe they need passports to get out of Greece. They might have found out about Dimitri's studio and asked him to insert their photographs on the stolen passports."

"But three passports were stolen," Zoe pointed out, "and there were only two people in the cave."

Mick snapped his fingers. "But there were three knapsacks! One guy could've been out running an errand or swimming or something."

"That's possible," Nancy agreed. "Someone went through the hotel safe and carefully selected the ID of two American men and one American female—that could match the group hiding in the cave. And Officer Rossolatos told us that American passports are highly valued in the underworld."

"Wait a minute," Bess said, swallowing hard. "Are you saying that the woman from the cave is going to escape the police by using *my* passport?"

"Possibly," Nancy said. "But she and the others need to have the photo page altered first. That's why I think there has to be a talented forger at work somewhere on these islands."

As Nancy described their trip to the police station, she remembered the word that the Greek police had kept using. *"Diafevgo,"* she said, turning to Zoe. "I hope I'm saying it right. Can you tell me what it means?"

"It's the Greek word for 'flee' or 'escape,'" Zoe said thoughtfully. "Maybe they were relieved that you and Mick escaped from those people."

Still not satisfied, Nancy said, "That might be

it—but it seemed like something was going on. I wonder if the police have had dealings with those people with the explosives before."

"Too bad Zoe wasn't at the police station to translate," Mick remarked.

"Or in the cave," Nancy added. "The man in the cave kept saying something . . . *shara*. What does that mean?" she asked Zoe.

Zoe shook her head. "It's not a Greek word."

The table was silent for a moment as everyone considered Nancy and Mick's close call. Then George said, "Nan, don't tell me you're going back to Dragonisi to look for that couple."

Nancy shook her head. "No way—not with those explosives lying around. I thought it would be wiser to wait for the police to check out that cave. Unfortunately, they didn't find anything."

"Nothing?" Bess asked incredulously.

"Hardly a trace," Zoe put in. "I called the police just before we left the hotel. They found the cave Nancy and Mick described, but the only thing left behind was the remnants of their campfire. They must have moved—and fast."

"Not a good sign," Nancy said, wincing. "They're on the run. I think we've stumbled into some serious trouble here."

"What are you going to do, Nan?" Bess asked.

"Keep an eye on Dimitri. If he's the forger, he might lead us to the others involved. There's one other person who concerns me, too." Nancy told them her suspicions about Theo.

Kevin scooped up the last bit of *souvlákia* on his plate, then looked at Nancy. "Let me get this straight. You think Zoe's friend Theo is helping those people with the explosives?"

"I don't know," Nancy said, "but so far, a lot of evidence points to it. Besides the cushions, I think I saw him talking with the red-haired woman who chased us from the cave. I want to check out his boat as soon as I can."

Zoe was dubious. "I've known Theo for many years. We tease him about how he'll do anything for money, but that's a joke. He would never help criminals."

"Maybe he doesn't know they're criminals," Mick pointed out.

"It just doesn't sound like Theo," Zoe insisted stubbornly. "I don't know what he was doing on Dragonisi, but he's never been interested in snorkeling before. I think you're wrong," she told Nancy, raising her chin.

Not wanting to argue with Zoe, Nancy let the subject drop. But if Theo wasn't a snorkeling fan, what was he doing with that group of divers?

After dinner the group walked along the waterfront to one of Chora's discos, which featured a circular dance floor and a live band.

The walls seemed to throb with the loud drumbeat of rock music as Nancy took her seat at the table. Within minutes George and Kevin were among the young people on the crowded dance floor. Two tables were taken up by a soccer team from Germany, and a few of the guys came over to talk to Zoe and Bess.

Nancy and Mick had danced through half a

dozen rock songs when Nancy decided she needed a breath of fresh air. She and Mick made their way out to a small garden terrace. Zoe was already there, she saw, drinking a soda.

"Trying to escape the party animals?" Nancy teased, trying to ease the tension that had cropped up between Zoe and her over Theo.

Zoe nodded. "Just for a moment. It's such a beautiful night."

As a light breeze ruffled her hair, Nancy had to agree. The sweet scent of jasmine filled the air, and the moon cast a milky glow over the mulberry trees along the patio.

"Looks like there's a full moon tonight," Mick observed, staring up at the bright disk that lit up the island.

"A good night for sleuthing." Nancy hesitated, looking at Zoe, before adding, "I'll bet I'd be able to find my way around Theo's boat without a flashlight."

Mick's flashing eyes told Nancy that he seconded the idea. Zoe was a little hesitant, but in the end she agreed. "As long as you let me come along," she insisted. "If we run into trouble, I might be able to talk our way out of it."

Nancy followed Zoe out through a back door that led to a narrow lane. "The marina is just a few blocks away, and we won't be gone long," Zoe said. "I don't think the others will miss us."

Although cafés along the waterfront were alive with customers, the harborside marina was quiet. Nancy soon spotted the *Sea Star* bobbing gently in its slip. The boat looked dark and deserted.

"It'll go faster if we split up," Nancy suggested as they approached the boat.

Mick nodded. "I'll check out the cabin below. You two can cover the main deck."

As Mick disappeared into the tiny cabin, Nancy and Zoe searched the aft deck. Zoe found that the bench seats below the orange cushions opened up. Inside were life jackets, extra rope, and two flare guns for use in an emergency.

Then they moved to the deck in front of the cabin, where they checked the cabinet below the steering column and found a flashlight and a tackle box.

"Hey," Mick called softly from the doorway of the cabin. "Check this out." He held up a weathered book with entries scrawled on the pages.

Zoe took the book and leafed through it. "It's the ship's log," she explained.

"Does it say anything about Theo's trips to Dragonisi?" Nancy asked.

Zoe nodded. "He's been traveling to Dragonisi a lot—nearly every day. But it doesn't say what he's doing there."

Bringing supplies to criminals? thought Nancy. The people from the cave would need food, fresh water, and news from the outside. Was Theo their tie to the rest of the world?

After Zoe explained the log entries, Mick went belowdeck to replace the book. He had just reappeared on the deck, when Nancy heard footsteps on the dock.

"Get down!" she whispered urgently.

Mick hunched on the right side of the cabin

while Nancy and Zoe squeezed behind the steering column. Peering around, Nancy saw Theo walking along the dock toward his boat. A ring of keys jingled in one hand.

"It's Theo!" Nancy reported.

Zoe sank back against the boat's control panel. "The one person I don't want to try to explain this to. Nancy, don't let him find me here, please!"

But it was too late. Theo was already at the edge of the dock. He whistled as he leapt onto the deck beside the cabin—just around the corner from Mick's hiding place!

Chapter

Ten

NANCY BIT HER LIP as Theo landed on the deck on the far side of the cabin, his weight making the boat rock slightly. There had to be a way to stall him—even distract him. Pressed against the steering column, she remembered the flashlight stowed below it, and an idea came to mind.

"Get ready to jump onto the next boat," she whispered to Zoe, pointing to the rickety fishing boat that was moored next to the *Sea Star*.

While Theo collected cushions from the aft deck, Nancy reached into the cabinet and grabbed the flashlight. Staying low, she moved silently along the deck to the front of the cabin. Then she switched the flashlight on and rolled it along the deck on the left side of the cabin, opposite Mick.

Although she couldn't see Theo, she heard his whistling stop. Peeking around the cabin, she saw him moving toward the rolling flashlight, which made a clumping noise as the beam of light skittered across the boat.

Her plan had worked!

Quickly Nancy scrambled to the opposite side of the cabin and followed Mick, who was already leaping onto the next boat. They clambered for cover under a tarp and huddled beside Zoe, the three of them breathless as they listened to Theo mutter aloud in confusion.

Zoe covered her mouth to suppress a giggle. "Poor Theo," she whispered. "He's wondering if his boat is haunted!"

After Theo went inside his boat's cabin, Nancy, Mick, and Zoe quickly exited the neighboring boat and headed back toward the disco. As they walked, Mick reported that he had found nothing unusual belowdeck. "There was just fishing gear, a black wet suit, and lots of snorkeling equipment."

Zoe had mentioned that Theo had never been interested in snorkeling before, Nancy remembered. So why did he suddenly have all this equipment? Seeing the closed, defensive expression on Zoe's face, however, Nancy decided not to bring that up now.

"Nothing on the boat really explains what Theo is doing on Dragonisi every day," Mick said.

"I wonder if any of the other fishermen know what he's been up to?" Nancy said thoughtfully.

Zoe hesitated, as if making a decision. "I can ask them—in a subtle way—tomorrow morning when I go into Chora to buy seafood for the inn," she volunteered. "I hate to spy on Theo, but if he's involved with those dangerous people, I want to know about it."

When they reached the disco, Zoe waved toward the hillside behind the building. Nancy saw the silhouette of a windmill at the top of the incline. "It's such a beautiful night," Zoe told Mick and Nancy. "You two should climb Kato Myli Hill and get a closer look at the windmills."

"I did want to get a chance to see them," Nancy admitted.

"Then go," Zoe insisted. "It's a very romantic walk." She showed them the lane that led to the short stairway at the base of the hill. "I'll tell the others. See you back at the hotel," she said, then pushed past the crowd on the steps of the disco.

Following Zoe's directions, Nancy and Mick walked past a sprawling white church built in the Cycladic style of the islands. "It looks like a giant cream puff," Mick observed.

Nancy laughed and looped her arm through his. She always felt so . . . relaxed with Mick. It felt very natural to work out a mystery with him.

A short climb up the stairway brought them to the top of the hill. They paused at the foot of the first white windmill and stared up at the canvas and wood sails, which turned lazily in the breeze.

"Just think," Nancy said dreamily. "These windmills have greeted thousands of people . . . rock stars, famous actors, ambassadors . . ."

"And top-notch detectives," Mick added, cradling Nancy's face with his hands. He placed a gentle kiss on her lips, and Nancy felt a tingle pass from head to toe.

"Right now I don't feel like an ace detective," she admitted. Sitting on the pedestal of one of the windmills, she added, "We really need a break in this case—like tracking down that couple from the cave. I wonder what they plan to do with those explosives?"

"That detective's mind is ticking away again," Mick said, slipping an arm around Nancy's shoulders. "You're remarkable, Nancy. I have to admit, I'm falling in love with you."

His words took her breath away. Searching her heart, Nancy knew that she felt the same way about Mick. But how could they have fallen in love in such a short time? "Oh, Mick, we've only known each other for—"

"I know, just two months," he interrupted. "And I know I've been hinting around about a trip to Australia. But the truth is, I'm not talking about a chartered tour. I'd like to take you back to Australia as my bride."

In that instant Nancy felt the entire world screech to a halt. All she could do was stare at Mick in shock.

"Bride?" she finally managed to say. *Bride,* as in wedding, as in married to Mick forever . . . for better or worse? Nancy's heart raced with the most magical, terrifying feeling she had ever experienced.

"Don't look so shocked," Mick said, running a

finger along her chin. "Two people who love each other should be together. Usually it makes them happy," he teased.

Nancy struggled to put her feelings into words. "It isn't that," she said. "I love being with you, Mick. It's just that I wasn't thinking about getting married." Suddenly an image shot into her head. She closed her eyes and tried to imagine leaving her hometown . . . saying goodbye to her dad and to Hannah Gruen, their housekeeper, who had helped take care of her when she was growing up.

"Well, will you think about it?" he asked.

"Of course," Nancy promised. Framed by moonlight, Mick's face looked so handsome. Leaning toward her, he covered her mouth in a kiss that Nancy was sure would melt her heart forever.

"Married!" Bess shrieked when Nancy returned to the room and filled her friends in on Mick's proposal.

"What did you say?" George asked.

Nancy sank down onto her bed. "I didn't want to hurt his feelings, so I told him I'd think about it," she said. "I have to admit, I'm crazy about the guy, but—"

"You're thinking about Ned, right?" asked Bess.

"Yes," Nancy admitted. "There's also River Heights, my detective work, Dad—and you guys. How can I leave all that behind?"

Bess went over to Nancy's bed and gave her a

hug. "If you decide to marry Mick and go to live in Australia, we'll come visit you, that's all. Nothing should come between two people who are in love!"

"The wise one has spoken," George said. Giving Nancy a sympathetic smile, she said, "It's a question that only you can answer. I mean, I really care about Kevin, but I'm not sure that I'd be crazy about the idea of following him around the world." She shrugged. "It's a tough call."

That was for sure, Nancy thought. She resolved not to make any decision right away. But that night Nancy fell asleep dreaming of the rambling sheep ranches and vast beaches of Australia.

"I looked for Theo this morning, at the harbor," Zoe told Nancy the next morning as they took a hydrofoil to Naxos, the largest of the Cyclades islands. They had been late boarding the craft, so Mick, Bess, and George had found scattered seats among the other thirty or so passengers.

Nancy pulled her orange hat lower on her head to ward off the sun. It was just before ten, but even in her shorts and tank top, she could feel the heat. "Any luck?" she asked Zoe.

"The *Sea Star* was already gone. Some of the fishermen say they've seen Theo anchored near Dragonisi. They thought he was fishing, but he's been coming in without a catch for the past week."

What does he do on Dragonisi if he's not fishing? Nancy wondered. She didn't have time to pursue the subject. Just then the engines slowed, and the hydrofoil docked in the bustling capital of Naxos.

From the terminal, the island looked like a mixture of whitewashed villages and lush green valleys. As soon as they were on land, Zoe suggested mopeds to make it easier to get around.

"Definitely," said Bess. "We rented them when we were in Rome, and they were great."

Ten minutes later they had rented three large mopeds from a shop across from the ferry terminal. Zoe and Bess teamed up on one bike, Nancy and Mick shared another, and Kevin and George took the third.

Clustered together outside the moped shop, studying a map of the island, the group decided to make the Temple of Apollo their first stop.

Zoe and Bess led the way to the north side of the port, turning left from the ferry terminal. In single file the mopeds buzzed along a causeway that connected the main island to a tiny islet. As they rounded a curve, a gigantic stone post-and-lintel came into view.

"That must be the temple," Nancy said. A moment later Mick pulled into a parking lot teeming with vendors and tourists.

"This is the Temple of Apollo," Zoe said as they all clambered off the bikes. "That doorway is called the *Portora,* which means 'Great Door.'"

Staring up at the huge marble monument, Bess said, "That makes sense."

Even the swarm of tourists couldn't diminish

the enormous power of the ancient structure. As the group strolled around, Nancy saw a familiar-looking man cross the marble floor of the temple.

"I can't believe it," she told Mick in an undertone. "Dimitri is here."

Mick followed her gaze to the photographer, who had stopped to take a candid shot of a tiny girl.

"I wonder what he's doing here?" Nancy asked thoughtfully. After the previous day's discoveries, she had begun to think of Dimitri as the forger and Theo as the messenger. Could Dimitri's presence here have anything to do with the passports? "Let's split up, so we're less conspicuous," she suggested to the others.

"Good idea," George said. She pointed to a vendor's cart near the temple steps. "We'll meet you back at that ice cream stand in an hour."

Nancy was so busy watching Dimitri that she barely looked at the tan-colored marble ruins. He worked his charms on tourist after tourist, but she didn't see any kind of exchange or unusual encounter.

After the hour had elapsed, Nancy rejoined her friends by the temple steps. Bess and Zoe wanted to move on, but Nancy hesitated. She didn't want to leave Dimitri.

"George and I will keep an eye on him," Kevin volunteered. "You guys go ahead."

Nancy started to object, but Bess interrupted. "Great! We'll see you later." Nancy looked at Bess quizzically but said nothing.

"No problem," George said.

They arranged to meet for a late lunch in a popular taverna in the village. Then Bess, Zoe, Nancy, and Mick headed back toward their mopeds.

"Didn't you get it?" Bess said to Nancy. "They want to be alone," she went on dreamily, "to squeeze every bit of romance out of their last days together."

Nancy laughed. "I should have guessed you'd pick up on that."

"Too bad Kevin has to fly off to Madrid on Sunday," Zoe said.

As Nancy climbed on the moped and wrapped her arms around Mick's waist, she wondered again what the future held for Mick and her. Did they belong together—forever?

The rest of the morning passed quickly as they rode along the twisting roads of Naxos, passing sparkling white churches and crumbled ruins at every turn. They even saw a goat farmer who was moving his herd, the metallic clang of the goats' bells filling the air.

Just outside town they pulled off the road at a scenic overlook. Bess and Zoe sat down on a bench as Nancy walked to the edge of the cliff. Pushing back the brim of her orange cap, Nancy took in the view of silvery green olive trees stretching in rows along the hills next to the clustered white buildings of the village.

"Isn't it beautiful?" Mick asked, coming up next to her.

"It really is," Nancy said, and leaned contentedly against him.

The moment was broken soon after by the buzz of a moped. Turning, Nancy saw a silver moped with two people on it round the curve of the road.

The sun glinted off the chrome of the bike, blinding Nancy for a moment. She blinked, then gasped as she saw the face of the driver. An angry red scar ran from his chin to his ear.

It's the man from Dragonisi! Nancy thought, recoiling. There was no telling what he would do if he recognized them!

Chapter

Eleven

I T'S THEM!" Nancy exclaimed.

In the next instant she ducked behind the trunk of an olive tree, pulling Mick along with her. She winced as bark scraped against her bare arm, but she had to stay hidden.

"What's going on?" Mick asked, looking at Nancy as if she had lost her mind.

"The man from the cave is driving that moped," Nancy said breathlessly. "But I think we ducked out of sight before he saw us."

Hearing the sound of the motor fade, Nancy dared a look. The moped was just disappearing down the hillside in the direction of town. "I'd love to know where he's off to in such a hurry," she said, rubbing the chafed skin on her arm.

"Are you okay?" Bess asked, rushing over with Zoe. "What's going on?"

Nancy told them about the driver of the silver moped. She felt so helpless. How could she let those guys just ride on by?

"What about the man on the back?" Zoe asked.

"I don't know who he is," Nancy said, "but I can't stand to stay here when they might lead us to some answers. What if they're on their way to pick up the passports from Dimitri?"

Mick was already striding to their moped. "It's a long shot," he said, "but it's worth checking out."

"Don't be crazy!" Zoe protested, grabbing Nancy by the hand. "It's too dangerous."

"I don't think he recognized us," Nancy said. "But just to be safe, we'd better take off our hats—they're the same ones we had on at Dragonisi." She tossed her orange hat to Bess, while Mick gave his to Zoe. Then Nancy hopped onto the moped and slid her arms around Mick's waist.

"Don't worry," Mick said. "We'll stay out of sight. We're just going to observe." Before Zoe and Bess could say another word, he revved the moped's engine and steered onto the road.

"We'll meet you at the taverna!" Bess called after them. "And be careful!"

Nancy held on tight as Mick maneuvered the moped around a series of snaking curves. With these treacherous roads, she was afraid that they would never catch up with the two men. Then the moped's engine whirred as they reached a straight stretch of road, and Mick shifted into high gear.

Nancy's heart raced as she spotted the silver moped ahead on the road. "There they are!" she shouted.

"Let's drop back," Mick said, shifting into low gear to slow their bike.

To Nancy's relief, the men never glanced back. "I don't think they're even aware of us," she told Mick.

It was an easy drive over the open road, but Nancy's nerves were tense with anticipation. What if the two men met with Dimitri—or Theo? If she and Mick interfered, the results could be deadly.

Once they reached the outskirts of town, the chase became complicated by the narrow, zigzagging streets scattered with people, carts, and animals.

"We're losing them," Nancy said, wincing as a young girl with a basket darted in front of their bike, forcing Mick to veer away.

Mick drove with caution, but it cost them. "I can't keep up with them in these congested streets." He rolled to a stop as a pair of burros hauled a wagon into the center of the street, blocking the way.

Disappointed, Nancy pushed her hair out of her eyes and frowned. "Oh, well. Better safe than sorry."

At last the donkeys moved on, and Mick steered the moped onto a wider street. They were back at Naxos's main square now, Nancy realized, near the ferry terminal. The square was filled with tourists and merchants rushing to do business before the afternoon siesta. It was like a crazed obstacle course.

"Let's get away from this traffic," Mick said, taking a sharp turn down a narrow alley.

Neither he nor Nancy saw the silver moped careening toward them until the last second. "Look out!" Nancy screamed, bracing herself for the impact.

Mick managed to steer away from the silver moped, but the motion sent their bike skidding to the side. It nearly slid out from under them as the silver moped zoomed off.

A cloud of dust rose around them as Nancy and Mick struggled to regain their balance and finally wobbled to a stop. "You okay?" Mick asked, turning back toward Nancy.

"Fine," she said. But a moment later her nerves twanged as she looked up into the eyes of the man with the scar. The silver moped had circled back, Nancy saw, and it was just a few yards away. The man with the scar was standing next to the bike, staring at Nancy and Mick. Nancy caught a quick glimpse of the man on the bike. He was thin, with dark hair and a full beard.

Oh, no! Nancy thought. The man with the scar had recognized them from Dragonisi!

"What now?" Mick muttered through clenched teeth.

Before Nancy could answer, the man hopped back on the moped and revved the engine. The silver bike sped away into the square.

"Come on," Nancy said, getting off the bike and following on foot. She had gone only a few steps when the bike disappeared around a corner. With all of the activity in the square, there was no way she and Mick could follow them now.

Nancy let out a frustrated sigh. Not only had the crooks lost her and Mick before they could find out where they were going, but two very dangerous people knew who she and Mick were. "This case is definitely heating up," Nancy said under her breath. "I just hope we don't get burned!"

Lunch was a loud affair. The taverna Zoe had suggested was filled with a spirited crowd of students and tourists. Nancy tried a dish of lamb and vegetables wrapped in crispy pastry leaves called *filo*. While everyone ate, she and Mick filled them in on the commotion in the market square.

"Sounds like we missed a pretty dramatic scene," Kevin commented.

"It really got out of hand." Mick shook his head, looking miserable. "I can't believe we blew our cover *and* let those guys slip away."

"It's not your fault," Nancy said, touching Mick's hand. Then she turned to George. "How did it go with Dimitri?" She still needed evidence to connect him to the people with the explosives.

"Did you see him talk to a woman with red hair—"

"Or two guys—one bearded, one scar-faced?" Mick added hopefully.

Unfortunately, George and Kevin had nothing to report. From what they'd seen, it looked as if Dimitri had come to Naxos to make some money photographing tourists—nothing more.

Later that afternoon, when Nancy spotted Dimitri on the hydrofoil headed back to Mykonos, she decided to confront him. She doubted that he would actually confess to forgery, but with a little pressure he might let some useful information slip out.

She found him waiting in line at the hydrofoil's snack bar. "I have a confession to make," she told him. "Remember how I wanted to see your studio?"

Dimitri's dark eyes narrowed suspiciously. "Yes . . .?"

"Well, I just couldn't resist." Nancy hesitated as color rose in Dimitri's face. "One day when you were out, I sneaked in and checked out the equipment."

The photographer slammed his hand on the snack bar counter. "That was a stupid thing to do! You could have been hurt."

"Of course, I didn't touch anything," Nancy lied, surprised that Dimitri was so upset.

"That's not the point," he said. He motioned Nancy to a corner by the snack bar so that no one could overhear their conversation. "You must stay away from the studio," he said emphatically. "The truth is, it doesn't really belong to me. My friend lets me use it."

Nancy shot him a dubious look. "And all the fancy equipment," she persisted. "Does that belong to your *friend,* too?"

Dimitri nodded. "My friend—Spiros. He owns the stationery shop right below the studio."

All at once, Nancy felt her investigation shifting. Spiros? Was Dimitri lying to her? She couldn't be sure. He was obviously upset, but that would be natural if he had just learned that she was closing in on his forging operation.

"And what does Spiros use the equipment for?" Nancy asked.

Dimitri shrugged. "Please don't tell your friend, the one with the blond hair and the pretty smile," he asked.

"Bess?" Nancy said. "Does this have something to do with her passport?"

"Passport?" Dimitri raked his fingers through the dark curls over his brow and looked confused. "No, no. Please don't tell her that the studio isn't mine. I lied about it to impress her," he said. "Does she ever mention me?" he asked hopefully.

Nancy didn't know if he was serious or if he was just trying to throw her off the track. Dimitri *was* attentive to Bess whenever they met. Not knowing what to think, Nancy made an excuse to Dimitri and went back to her seat.

When she told everyone what she'd just

learned, Mick had an inspiration. "Spiros makes miniatures, doesn't he? I mean, didn't you buy a tiny windmill from him?" When Bess nodded, he added, "He probably uses the equipment to help with his sculptures."

"But you saw those machines, Mick," Nancy said. "They were pretty sophisticated—not just arts and crafts stuff. I'm not sure I trust Dimitri, but if Spiros really owns the equipment, he could be our forger."

"Not Spiros," Zoe objected. "I've known him since I was a child. He and my father are good friends. He has been like an uncle to me." She shook her head. "This has gone too far! First you suspect our maid, then my friend Theo, and now Spiros," she said, her voice cracking with strain.

"I'm sorry," Nancy said. She didn't want to hurt Zoe's feelings, but she had to follow the trail of clues if she wanted to get to the bottom of the passport theft.

"This is the perfect way to end the day," Bess said later that evening. She swayed to the strains of *bouzouki* music that was piped into the hotel's taverna. "What do the words mean?" she asked Zoe.

"The lyrics to most Greek songs are about love," Zoe explained.

Bess sighed. "It figures. That's probably why I'm crazy about Greek music."

A ballad began, and Nancy and Mick got up to dance. He swept her across the dance floor and twirled her under a trellis covered with fragrant hibiscus. Nancy felt as if she were floating on a cloud. Then a stern-looking young man appeared at the terrace door. He stopped a waiter, who pointed toward Nancy and Mick.

"Looks like we have a visitor," Nancy whispered into Mick's ear.

Mick turned his head and stared at the man in the doorway. "Looks serious," he said. He took Nancy's hand, and they went over to the edge of the terrace, where the young man was standing.

As it turned out, the man was a diplomatic courier. "I have a package for you from Thomas McCurdy," the courier said, handing Mick a thin manila envelope. After Mick thanked him, the courier disappeared as suddenly as he had arrived.

"What is it?" Nancy was dying of curiosity as she followed Mick back to the table.

"McCurdy is my father's friend—the ambassador in Athens that I mentioned before. This must be some information on Bess's stolen passport," Mick said as he broke the wax seal on the envelope.

Everyone leaned forward as Mick pulled out a letter and began to read in silence. A moment later he stopped and shook the envelope. Three glossy photographs spilled out—headshots of two men and a woman.

The air was heavy as the group stared at the photos. "That looks like the two guys you chased on Naxos today," Bess said, pointing to two of the pictures.

"And that's the redheaded woman who was in the cave on Dragonisi," Nancy said.

"What does the letter say?" Kevin wanted to know.

Mick looked soberly around the table. "That these people are terrorists," he replied, "and we should avoid them at all costs!"

Chapter

Twelve

An AUDIBLE GASP rose from the table. Nancy's heart plummeted as she realized just how deadly the situation she and Mick had stumbled into was.

"Terrorists!" George echoed, looking scared. "Nancy, you've been tangling with killers!"

"What else does the letter say about the terrorists?" Kevin asked.

Mick smoothed the sheet of crisp bond paper, summarizing as he read on. "They're three fugitives from the Middle East—explosives experts who were sent to prison for planting a bomb at a train station. The men are named Mashti and Rashid, and the woman is Shara—"

"That's it—Shara!" Nancy interrupted. "The guy in the cave kept saying it over and over. I guess he was just calling her."

111

"That's right," Mick said. Then he returned to reading the letter. "All three of them received life sentences, but two weeks ago they escaped from prison, killing two guards in the process."

With a shiver, Bess said, "Escaped prisoners? I can't believe Zoe and I let you go after them."

"Escaped . . ." Zoe said, thinking aloud. "Maybe that's why you heard the police saying *diafevgo* over and over—it's the Greek word for 'escape.' They probably realized that you had come face-to-face with these escaped prisoners but didn't want to scare you with the truth."

"Why would the police keep it a secret?" asked Bess.

Zoe frowned. "This kind of news could scare off visitors and harm the tourist trade. The police are probably trying to keep it quiet."

"But they've probably tightened security," Nancy said. "I'll bet that's why they were checking passports on Delos."

Mick tapped the manila envelope in front of him. "McCurdy thinks the terrorists have been moving around the islands in a stolen boat," he added. "But they need papers to leave the country."

"So our theory about the three stolen passports may be right," Nancy said. "It looks as if they're going to fall into the hands of these three criminals."

"Wow," Bess said, her eyes wide. "I feel like I've created an international incident."

"According to this letter, even Interpol is in on the case," said Mick. "They're compiling a special list of all lost or stolen passports in the hope that they'll be able to use it to snag the terrorists."

"Do you think we should go to the police with our suspicions of Theo and Dimitri?" George asked.

Nancy took a sip of her fruit drink, and thought for a moment. "We still don't have enough evidence."

"She's right," Mick added. "All we can do is watch and wait."

"And lay low," Kevin added.

Zoe nodded her agreement. "Now that the terrorists can identify Nancy and Mick, we should all be extra careful."

"I'm glad we weren't planning a trip for tomorrow," Bess said. "We'll be better off sticking around here."

The next morning everyone else was already on the beach by the time Nancy finished breakfast and changed into her suit. As she walked down the path toward the water, she saw Bess and George posing on beached Windsurfers for Dimitri. The photographer was kneeling in the sand, taking their picture. Dressed in a black wet suit, he looked more like a diver than a photographer.

"I will have all your photos back to you tomorrow," Dimitri promised Bess, smiling as he strapped the bright yellow waterproof camera around his neck. "But now I must meet a group of British tourists who have hired me. They want me to take photos of them snorkeling so they can brag to their friends back home."

As Dimitri headed off down the beach, Bess walked over to the beach towel where Nancy had just sat down. "I'm afraid to see those photos he took of me that afternoon in Chora when you guys searched his studio. It was such a hot day—I probably look awful."

"All in the line of duty," Nancy teased, her eyes on Dimitri's retreating form. Was his friendly smile just a cover-up for a master forger? Were he and Theo working together?

She lay down on her stomach. She was thinking about how to proceed with her investigation when she felt a splash of cold water on her back. She rolled over and sat up just as Mick tossed a snorkeling mask onto the beach towel beside her.

"Time for a dip, Nancy," he teased. "There are some amazing fish out there today."

"You're on, Devlin," Nancy said. Grabbing the mask, she raced him to the clear turquoise water.

With the help of the snorkeling gear, she spent the next half hour exploring the underwater world of the Aegean Sea. A school of tiny silvery fish fluttered past her, tickling her legs as they went. Lingering over a clump of seaweed, she discovered fish in dazzling shades of blue, orange, and yellow. She carefully avoided a group of pincushiony sea urchins, whose spines could sting.

Mick was just pointing out a tiny gray octopus

when Nancy caught sight of a diver out of the corner of her mask.

Turning her head, she saw that he was wearing a black wet suit, mask, and scuba-diving equipment—she couldn't make out his features at all. Nancy was about to look away when she noticed a strange contraption in the diver's arm. It looked like a cross between a rifle and an archery bow.

A second look made her gasp. The man was holding an underwater spear gun!

Grabbing Mick's arm, Nancy twisted around in the water to point out the armed diver.

Just then the diver aimed the gun and fired! With a burst of bubbles, a sharp spear torpedoed straight toward Nancy and Mick!

Chapter
Thirteen

NANCY FELT her whole body go tight. Pressing her hands against Mick's side, she pushed—as hard as one could push underwater—sending him in one direction while she moved in the other. A split second later she felt a rush of water as the spear zoomed past her.

Mick's arms flailed for a moment. Then Nancy saw him start swimming off in the opposite direction from the diver. Following his lead, she kicked frantically through the water behind him.

Quickly she turned back to see if another spear was coming her way. The masked diver was loading another one!

Without a moment to waste, she and Mick pushed above the surface and swam, trying to put distance between them and the diver. Nancy knew that they could move more quickly if they weren't under the surface, but with every stroke she took she thought about the sharp end of that spear.

Her muscles were screaming from exertion when she ducked her head under the water to check on the man with the spear gun. She was just in time to see the second spear veer off to her left. Then the diver turned and swam away from them.

Breaking through the surface, Nancy took a deep breath. "That was close," Mick said, coughing as he propped his mask on his head. "Did you get a look at that guy?"

Nancy pulled off her own snorkeling gear. "No, but there he is again!"

The diver had surfaced near a small motorboat that was floating some twenty yards away. Nancy watched as he tossed the spear gun into the boat, then heaved himself aboard. His head was covered with the black hood of a diver's suit, but Nancy was able to see that he was a man of medium build. A moment later the boat's engine roared to life, and the masked man sped away.

"Guess he's not going to stick around for a chat," Mick said, smiling weakly.

"No, but I think his message was clear. Someone wants us out of the picture." Nancy frowned. "I just wish I knew who that someone was."

When Nancy and Mick finally waded to shore, they found their friends playing cards, oblivious to what had transpired out in the sea.

"I can't believe all that action was going on while we were sitting here," Bess said, brushing sand from her legs.

"It's a good thing both you and Mick are good swimmers," George said, scanning the nearby water.

"Thank goodness you weren't hurt," Zoe added.

Nancy combed her wet hair and pulled it back into a ponytail. "I just wish I had seen the face of that man with the spear gun."

"Well, let's think about it," Kevin said. "Who could get their hands on a black wet suit?"

Mick dried off, then pulled a blue T-shirt over his head. "Theo has one. I saw it stashed in the cabin of his boat."

"But no one has seen Theo all morning," Zoe said defensively. "Besides, you would have recognized the *Sea Star.*"

"He could have borrowed a boat from one of his friends at the marina," Nancy pointed out, then added, "But we also saw Dimitri wearing a wet suit just this morning."

George snapped her fingers. "That's right! A black wet suit. He could have jumped in a boat after he disappeared down the beach."

"But he said he'd been hired to spend the hour photographing some tourists underwater," Bess added. "That's why he was wearing the wet suit."

"We should check out his story, just to be sure," Nancy said.

Mick looked out over the sea, a serious expression darkening his handsome face. "Do you think that those criminals decided to come after us?" he asked after a moment.

Nancy winced. "I sure hope not. First of all, I'm not sure they'd be able to find us that easily. And if the police are looking for them, my guess is that they'd want to lay low."

"But it *is* a possibility," Bess said, her brow furrowed in concern. "I think we all need to be careful."

"I don't intend to mess with those terrorists again," Nancy assured her friends.

Just then she caught sight of a young man in a black wet suit coming down the path from the hotel. At first she was alarmed, but that feeling faded when she realized it was Theo. He waved and headed right for them.

"Theo's finally turned up," Nancy whispered to her friends, "and he's dressed for the part."

"Yásou!" Theo called out cheerfully. "I've just come back from Dragonisi. I caught a few fish this morning, too."

"Why are you wearing that?" Zoe snapped at him. She looked as if she didn't know whether she should attack or defend her friend.

Theo glanced down at the wet suit. "I was snorkeling," he said, confused.

"You *hate* snorkeling," Zoe retorted.

"I changed my mind," Theo said. He looked from Zoe to the others on the beach. "What's going on here? Why are you all so serious?"

Jumping to her feet, Zoe went nose-to-nose

with Theo. "Nancy and Mick were just attacked by a man with a spear gun—a man in a black wet suit."

"You must be joking!" he said. Then, realizing that they were serious, he said, "Wait a minute. You don't think that I—"

Zoe jabbed a finger at his chest. "And you've been spending a lot of time on Dragonisi—where three international terrorists were hiding out!"

"What?" Theo looked completely baffled. "What is she talking about?"

Although Nancy wasn't happy that Zoe had told Theo about the terrorists, she couldn't let the subject drop now. She told Theo about the letter from Mick's diplomat friend and about the cushions from the *Sea Star* that she and Mick had found in the terrorists' cave.

"I never met those people—I swear it," he insisted. "A lot of things have disappeared from my boat over the past few weeks. First there were the missing cushions, then fishing equipment and cans of food. I thought the other fishermen were playing tricks on me. Then I realized everything disappeared while I was anchored near Dragonisi."

"That explains about the orange cushions," Mick said to Nancy. "And the terrorists probably stole the canned food and fishing stuff, too."

Nancy still wasn't convinced. "But what about the red-haired girl?" she asked. Theo blanched at the question, but she didn't back off. "We saw you with a young woman—a petite girl with red hair who looked just like the female terrorist."

"She's not a terrorist!" Frustrated, Theo rubbed his hands over his eyes, then peeked out through his fingers at Zoe. "I have been taking snorkeling lessons from a diving instructor on Dragonisi. A pretty girl, a redhead. But her name is Eleni. And she would never hurt anyone."

"Then why is Eleni such a big secret?" George asked.

Nancy thought she knew the answer, but she waited for Theo's reply. Staring at Zoe, he said, "I didn't want to hurt you. I know you've been mad at me for breaking up, but I want to stay friends."

"I've been mad at you for acting so strange!" Zoe protested. "What kind of friend refuses to talk about what he does all day, every day?"

Theo shrugged. "I'm sorry. Will you forgive me?"

Zoe rolled her eyes and sighed. "Only if you promise to be honest with me from now on," she said. "And wipe that sheepish look off your face."

"I promise," Theo said, smiling.

Nancy was glad that Zoe was on better terms with her friend, but she knew that Theo couldn't be ruled out as a suspect yet. His explanations were reasonable, but how could she be sure that he was telling the truth?

"I don't understand how Dimitri can still be a suspect," Bess said as she toweled off her hair.

After a walk down the beach to check up on Dimitri's whereabouts, the girls had returned to their room to shower before lunch.

"She's right," George added. "Those British tourists said that Dimitri spent the entire morning with them, so he couldn't have been the guy with the spear gun."

"That proves he didn't attack us," Nancy said, "but Dimitri could still be the forger." Nancy slipped on a royal blue tank top and tucked it into her white denim miniskirt.

"What about Theo?" George asked. "Didn't you believe his explanation?"

Nancy let out a sigh. "I want to believe him," she said, pushing back her hair with a blue cloth headband. "But we can't be sure until we have proof—not just his word." She opened the wooden shutters to the balcony, and sunlight streamed into the room.

"I wish we knew who we were up against," Bess said.

"It's a dangerous situation for all of . . ." Nancy's voice trailed off. She was standing with her back to the balcony doorway. The sunlight that streamed in hit the top of the dresser, illuminating Bess's gift-wrapped package.

"Wait a minute," Nancy said, stepping over to the dresser. Because of the sunlight directly hitting the package, she could see tiny, squiggly blue lines on the wrapping paper.

"What's wrong?" George asked, standing up.

The intricately patterned blue-green wrapping paper looked familiar to Nancy. She picked up the package and looked more closely. She could make out an eagle in the center of the page. "That's it!"

She whirled toward Bess and George, who had paused in the middle of dressing to gaze at her. "The answer has been sitting right in this room for days."

"What are you talking about?" Bess asked.

Nancy waved the package in the air. "See the wrapping paper on this gift? When Dimitri wrapped it in Spiros's shop, he must have used the wrong paper. This is engraved with an eagle —just like the pages of a U.S. passport."

George hurried over to Nancy and grabbed the package. Bess moved in close to study it.

"That means Spiros could be the one who's forging the passports!" George exclaimed, looking up at Nancy in awe.

Nancy nodded. "Exactly."

Chapter

Fourteen

I CAN'T BELIEVE that clue was in our room all along—right under our noses," Bess said.

After she, Nancy, and George had shared their revelation with their friends, the group decided to talk over the case at lunch. Now they were at a small waterfront sandwich shop on the harbor in Chora.

"I am disappointed that my father's friend would steal from our hotel," Zoe said as a waitress brought a tray of iced lemonade to their table. "But if Spiros is the forger, the police should know about it."

Nancy took a long drink of lemonade. She was glad that Zoe understood the need to follow through on their suspecting Spiros.

"I don't get it," Kevin said. "How could Spiros

be so stupid as to wrap a gift in a fake passport page?"

"Spiros didn't do it," George explained. "Dimitri wrapped the gift while Spiros was out of the room."

"Which proves that Dimitri isn't involved in the passport forgery," Nancy added. "He would never have used that paper if he knew what it was intended for."

"I'll bet Spiros will be steaming mad when he figures out Dimitri's mistake," Mick said.

Nancy nodded. "I just wish I could figure out how Spiros got his hands on those stolen passports."

"I think he stole them himself—right from our safe," Zoe said grimly. Seeing Nancy's surprised expression, Zoe explained that Spiros had been visiting her father at the inn the morning the thefts occurred. "I forgot that he was there, since I never considered him a suspect."

"If you were opening and closing the safe as often as you said, it would have been easy enough for Spiros to see what the combination was. Then he probably opened it when you or your father were at the front desk," Nancy said.

Picking up on Nancy's thoughts, Mick said, "And since your father is so close to Spiros, he never suspected him, either."

Now that she had a target, Nancy felt a new sense of urgency. "I've got to find a way to catch Spiros red-handed—before he gives those passports to the terrorists. We need to watch him closely."

"I have a girlfriend who lives across the lane from Spiros's shop," Zoe explained. "She is away in Athens this week, but her balcony has an outside entrance, and we can use it to watch Spiros without being seen."

"Sounds perfect," Nancy said, picking up a piece of *tost,* a roll stuffed with spiced pork and pressed into a crispy toasted square.

Kevin passed the sandwich platter to George and asked, "Does this mean we're staging a stakeout?"

"I guess you could say that," Mick replied.

"But stakeouts can be boring," Nancy warned everyone, "especially when they drag on for hours. Maybe we should work in shifts to make it easier on everyone."

The others agreed that Nancy's idea was a good one. It was decided that Nancy and Mick would take the first watch after lunch. George and Kevin would relieve them an hour later, and Zoe and Bess would take the third shift.

"This balcony gives us a perfect view," Mick said. He was kneeling and peering over the waist-high ledge of the stucco balcony. The house that Zoe had brought him and Nancy to was just across the narrow lane from Spiros's shop. From the balcony they could look right into the windows of the studio and of the shop below it. All they had seen of Spiros so far was the top of his head in the store as he sat behind the counter, reading a magazine.

"I just hope we're not too late," Nancy said.

She was kneeling, too. She also hoped that George and Kevin would show up soon; her knees were getting sore.

"I don't think anything's happened yet," Mick said, giving Nancy's ankle a squeeze. "It's just a matter of time before this whole case is wrapped up. And then what? What's in store for us?"

Nancy glanced at his angular, rugged face. She leaned back, into a semisitting position. "I've been thinking about your proposal," she said slowly. "And I'd really love for you to show me Australia."

"Great!"

Before Mick could get carried away, she added, "But Australia is really far away. I'm just not sure about—"

"We can visit River Heights," Mick interrupted. *"After* you meet my parents. It'll be terrific, Nancy. You'll see."

"I haven't made a decision yet," Nancy said, holding up her hands.

"And I'm not rushing you," Mick told her. He dropped a kiss on her cheek.

"Are we interrupting something?" Bess asked from behind them. Turning, Nancy saw Bess and Zoe climbing the closed stairway to the balcony.

"We brought these binoculars from the inn," Zoe said, handing Nancy the glasses.

"We're going to get ice cream," Bess added. "Want us to bring you some?"

Nancy checked her watch. "George and Kevin will take over in ten minutes or so," she said. "I think we can hold out till then."

"Hey, look—he's leaving the shop," Mick whispered, nudging Nancy.

While Bess and Zoe ducked behind the balcony wall, Nancy peered over the top. Spiros was just locking up the shop. Then he climbed the stairs and entered the second-floor studio.

"I should have guessed," Nancy whispered excitedly. "He has time to work on the passports when the shop is closed for siesta." She and Mick watched as the old man moved about the room for a few minutes, then sat down at a worktable bathed in sunlight.

"What's he doing?" Mick asked after a few more minutes. "It looks as if he's sewing."

Looking through the binoculars, Nancy was able to make out the item on the table. "He *is* sewing. He's doing the seam of a passport!" The sight of the large darning needle sent her mind reeling back. "Remember the sewing basket I found in his file cabinet? That's what it's for!"

She handed the binoculars to Mick, who held them up, then whistled. "Pretty crafty."

"So it looks as if he's almost finished?" Bess asked.

Nancy nodded. "He must have taken the passport apart to remove the identification page— the one with the photo. Then all he has to do is duplicate a single page with a new photo and new information and sew it all back together."

They watched as Spiros finished his task and then tucked the passports into the sewing basket. Still holding the basket, he headed for the door.

"What do you think?" Mick asked Nancy.

"We know he's got the passports," she whispered. "Let's split up. We need to contact the police—and keep an eye on Spiros."

"I'll go for the police," Zoe volunteered.

Peering over the ledge, they watched Spiros tuck the basket in the crook of his arm. He went down the stairs and headed down the street. "Let's go," Nancy said.

The cobblestone lane was fairly deserted, so the teens followed Spiros at a distance. Most locals and tourists had retired indoors for a siesta. A few blocks down, Zoe turned off down a side street, which led to the police station.

As Nancy, Mick, and Bess followed Spiros through the twisting maze of streets, they passed a handful of Japanese tourists and a young boy with a goat. After a few minutes they found themselves at the foot of the staircase leading up to the windmills.

"This is it," Nancy said as she started up the stairs. "If he's got those passports, we have to get them now—before he sells them." She knew Spiros would never hand over the forged passports. She would have to catch him off guard.

Thinking of a plan, she reached into the back pocket of her denim skirt and pulled out her own passport, which she had carried with her ever since the day the safe was broken into. She had had no idea, then, just how handy her own passport would be!

At the top of the stairs, Nancy saw that Spiros

was the only person on the hot, dry summit of the hill. His eyes narrowed suspiciously as he spotted them.

Forcing a smile, Nancy held out her passport as she approached him. "We found this on the steps. I think it fell out of your basket."

Spiros's gaze fell on the passport in her hand. With its blue cover and gold seal, it could have been one of the forged passports. Spiros pulled his pipe out of his mouth, then slowly reached forward until his hand closed around Nancy's passport.

Before Spiros knew what had hit him, Nancy tugged the basket out of his grasp, and Mick grabbed his arms, to restrain him.

"We'll be needing this, too," Bess said, snatching Nancy's passport from Spiros's hand.

Nancy rummaged through the basket and pulled out the three passports, their covers bearing the U.S. seal. Nancy opened the first one and saw the face of the bearded terrorist staring at her. Inside the second one she saw the photo of the woman, Shara. "This must be Bess's passport," she said. Flipping through the pages, she saw the stamps they had gotten earlier that summer in Switzerland and Italy.

"Leave me alone!" Spiros shouted, struggling to get away from Mick. "You are crazy to be involved in this!"

"This is all the evidence we need!" Nancy announced, waving the passports as Mick wrestled Spiros down and pinned him to the ground.

"Do you want me to run down to the police

station?" Bess offered. "Zoe has no way of knowing that we wound up here."

"Good idea. And take these." Nancy handed Bess the three forged passports.

"I'll be back in a flash—with the police," Bess promised. Then she ran down the steps of Kato Myli Hill.

Spiros had given up struggling with Mick, but he let forth with a flood of angry Greek phrases.

Nancy slipped off her blue headband and gave it to Mick. "Use this on his arms." A moment later Spiros's wrists were bound, and he was sitting on the stone pedestal of one of the windmills, with Nancy and Mick standing on either side of him.

For several minutes no one spoke. Then Spiros said urgently, "Please. We must leave here— right away. We are all in danger."

"The police will be here any minute," Nancy said. She caught a flicker of movement out of the corner of her eye. "This must be them now."

Turning her head to peer around the side of the windmill, she heard a sudden cold click, then felt a small solid object against her temple.

Nancy drew in a sharp breath. She had heard that sound before. It was the sound of a cocked pistol—and it was pressed against the side of her head.

Her heart began to hammer in her chest, and she thought, One move and I'm dead.

Chapter

Fifteen

"Don't move," said a man with a deep, accented voice, as if he were reading her mind. Nancy didn't dare turn to look at him.

In the next instant she heard the metallic sound of another gun being cocked, and her heart sank. Mick was in danger, too!

Loud male voices growled in a language Nancy didn't understand. When she dared to glance slightly toward her right, she saw that Spiros was arguing with one of the terrorists, the scar-faced man. From studying the photos, Nancy remembered that his name was Mashti.

The other two, Shara and Rashid, stood nearby. The pistol at Nancy's head was held by Rashid, while Shara had her gun trained on Mick.

Spiros waved off Mashti defiantly, then pointed at Nancy. "Ask her," he spat, switching to English. "She can tell you where your passports went."

Nancy felt her mouth go dry as the muscular Mashti lunged toward her and yanked her arm.

"Hand over the passports—now!" he demanded.

"I don't have them," Nancy said. She wasn't about to let them know that Bess was on her way to the police station with them at that very moment.

"Ah, but she can get them," Spiros objected.

Infuriated, Mashti kicked up a puff of dust, then pressed his face close to Nancy's. The hair on her neck stood on end as his hot breath brushed her skin. "You are going to get those passports for me—if you want to live."

Nancy saw a sudden movement behind him, and she realized that someone was coming. The police—at last, she thought.

A moment later she gasped in horror as she recognized George.

"There you are!" George cried. "Bess told us you were up here guarding—"

She stopped short, taking in the situation. "Whoa!" Kevin said, stopping next to her.

Mashti pulled out a revolver, whirled, dropped to a crouch, and trained the gun on Kevin and George. "Stop!" he shouted.

George and Kevin froze, their faces reflecting total shock. Quickly Mashti corralled them against the wall of the windmill so that they stood beside Nancy and Mick. One by one the terrorists patted down Nancy and her friends. Nancy suspected they were searching for weapons or the forged passports. They found nothing.

After a heated argument with Spiros, Mashti pulled Nancy away from the wall of the windmill.

"You will get the passports back," he ordered, shaking his fist in her face. "Bring the passports to the cave on Dragonisi—you know the one. You have three hours. Be there by six o'clock, or your friends will die." Then he backed away.

For a moment Nancy couldn't believe her eyes. The terrorists were letting her and Mick go free!

Then her heart sank as she saw them nudge George and Kevin with their guns, pushing them toward the stairs. They were going to use George and Kevin as hostages!

This can't be happening! Nancy thought. Tears filled her eyes as George flashed her a look of desperation, then turned away. Nancy watched, horrified, as the three terrorists descended the stairs, hurrying George and Kevin along at gunpoint.

"He says that he has forged passports many times in the past, but never before for anyone he thought was dangerous," Zoe murmured. "With him, forging is an art, like the miniature statues he makes." In a small, hot room of the police station, Zoe was translating Spiros's statement.

"The terrorists had heard of his reputation, and they threatened to kill him if he did not do as they asked," Zoe went on. She seemed disappointed in her family's friend, and Nancy didn't blame her. She guessed that it *was* an art to recreate something as intricate as a passport, but that didn't justify breaking the law.

Zoe and Officer Rossolatos had helped move things along quickly. Spiros was under arrest. Two men had been sent out to search Mykonos for the terrorists and their hostages—just in case they hadn't left the island yet. And the police chief had put in a call to Interpol, the international police network. The police would take action once Interpol arrived.

Officer Rossolatos allowed Nancy and the others to listen in while Spiros confessed to opening the hotel safe, stealing the passports, and altering them.

"This is all your fault!" Spiros scowled at Nancy. "If you had not stuck your nose in this business, your friends would be safe. I knew you were going to be a threat when Dimitri told me you had been in my studio. That is why I tried to frighten you while you were swimming."

"*You* were the man with the spear gun!" Nancy said as the pieces of the puzzle fell into place.

"Why didn't you back off when you still had the chance?" Spiros asked her. "I warned you!"

"Nancy isn't scared off by threats," Bess said, coming to Nancy's defense. Her eyes were red from crying.

But maybe this time I should have been, Nancy thought. She sank back in her chair, a sick feeling in her stomach. Spiros was right. If she had backed off, her friends' lives wouldn't be in jeopardy at this moment. What if the terrorists made good on their threat? Solving one case just wasn't worth two precious lives.

Once Spiros's statement was complete, Nancy, Bess, Zoe, and Mick were dismissed. "Thank you for your cooperation," the police chief said in a matter-of-fact way. Nancy had the feeling that he didn't understand how serious the situation was.

"What's going to happen to my friends?" she asked him anxiously. It was almost four o'clock. Minutes were ticking by, and George and Kevin were still in the hands of the terrorists.

Officer Rossolatos intervened, speaking to his supervisor in Greek. Then Rossolatos turned to Nancy and said, "We will send an Interpol agent who matches your description to the cave. She will trade the forged passports for your friends. Of course, after the trade, a team of officers will surround the terrorists. The criminals will surrender—if they want to live."

"And what if they refuse to release George and Kevin?" Nancy asked, blinking as her eyes filled with tears.

"Please," said the officer. "You must trust us to handle it."

That's no answer! Nancy wanted to shriek. A wave of guilt washed over her as she thought about the terrible situation she had gotten her friends into. She wished the police would use her instead of a decoy, but she knew they would never agree to it.

Turning to Bess, she asked, "Do you still have

my hat?" Nancy had given her orange cap to Bess before she and Mick rode off after the terrorists on Naxos.

"Sure," Bess said. She was still carrying the tote bag she'd had on Naxos. She reached into it and pulled out Nancy's fluorescent orange cap.

Nancy handed the hat to Officer Rossolatos. "I had this on when I first ran into the terrorists. The decoy might want to wear it."

"Thank you," he said. "We will contact you as soon as your friends are in our custody."

"And there's a six o'clock deadline!" Nancy stressed.

Rossolatos smiled reassuringly. "We will be there long before the deadline. Do not worry."

How could she help but worry?

Nancy was surprised to find Theo coming out of an office when she, Zoe, and Mick walked into the hall. Immediately there was an exchange in Greek between Theo and Zoe. "Theo came in to make a report," Zoe explained. "His boat was stolen from Mykonos's harbor. A few of the fishermen saw two men boarding the *Sea Star*. From their description, it sounds as if the two male terrorists stole the *Sea Star*. One of the fishermen remembers seeing a red-haired woman board a smaller boat."

"Was George with them?" Bess asked, but Theo didn't know.

"Why did they take your boat," Mick wondered, "when they had the other one?"

"Maybe they need a faster, larger boat than the one they've been using," Nancy suggested.

137

She followed her friends outside into the late afternoon sunshine. The bright sky seemed to contrast sharply with the darkness of her mood.

"Maybe we should go back to the hotel and wait," Zoe suggested bleakly.

"She's right," Bess said, wiping tears from her eyes. She couldn't stop crying. "There's really nothing else we can do."

"I can't just sit around and wait," Nancy said. "I'll go crazy."

"Don't tell me," Mick said, raising an eyebrow at her. "You want to go to Dragonisi?"

"I have to," Nancy told him.

"It's too dangerous," Bess insisted. "If the terrorists see us, they might kill George and Kevin on the spot."

Nancy frowned, thinking. "We can wait in a boat offshore, out of the way of the police and where the terrorists can't see us."

Zoe shook her head. "It's too risky."

"Please," Nancy pleaded. "I just need to be sure that George and Kevin get away safely."

"I can take you there," Theo offered. "A friend of mine at the marina told me that I could use his boat until I get mine back."

"Thanks," Nancy said gratefully. "We should leave right away. The six o'clock deadline isn't that far away—it's already four-thirty."

"This is crazy," Mick said hesitantly, "but I know there's no changing your mind. Count me in."

Bess and Zoe exchanged a look, then Zoe shrugged. "I guess I'm going to see Dragonisi, after all," Bess said, feeling miserable as she followed her friends down the street to the marina.

As Theo had promised, a small blue boat, similar in size to the *Sea Star,* awaited them at Mykonos's harbor. As Theo steered the boat out of the harbor, Bess sat beside Nancy on the aft deck. "I guess Theo's not a suspect anymore," Bess said.

Nancy nodded. "It looks as if the operation was directly between the terrorists and Spiros. The fact that the terrorists stole Theo's boat proves that he was just an innocent victim."

And so are George and Kevin, she added silently, staring out at the churning sea.

By the time they neared Dragonisi, it was already five-thirty. Just thirty minutes until the deadline, yet there wasn't a police vessel in sight.

"Something must be wrong," Nancy said as Theo cut the boat's engine offshore. They were behind a huge rock formation that jutted out of the water. By leaning over the forward deck, however, Nancy could see the cave entrance and the shore. Squinting, she could also see a yellow boat moored near the beach and a smaller boat. "Theo," Nancy asked, pointing, "isn't that your boat?"

Theo leaned forward. "That's the *Sea Star,* all right."

Nancy choked back a sick feeling. "What's keeping the police?"

"Maybe they're already inside," Bess said, but she looked just as worried as Nancy felt.

Nancy shook her head. "No. We'd see another boat—maybe more."

"Let's just sit tight and see what happens," Mick suggested. Nancy didn't see any alternative, so she and the others settled in by the forward railing. Their eyes were glued to the rocky beach.

"Those binoculars we used to watch Spiros might help," Bess said, pulling them out of her tote bag. "Here." She handed them to Theo.

Tense moments passed without a sign of another boat. The waiting is killing me, Nancy thought as she checked her watch yet again. Twenty minutes to the deadline!

"Someone's coming out of the cave!" Theo announced, handing Nancy the binoculars.

Nancy recognized Mashti, the muscular man. As she watched, he transferred the four cartons of explosives from the smaller boat to the *Sea Star.* "They're moving everything to Theo's boat," she said. A moment later Rashid came out and helped Mashti move knapsacks onto the *Sea Star.*

"They're getting ready to leave," Nancy told the others, lowering the field glasses. A tense silence settled over the group.

"Where are the police?" Mick finally said.

"No one has brought the passports," Nancy said anxiously. "The terrorists must be getting ready to kill George and Kevin! I've got to go in there—before it's too late."

Chapter

Sixteen

NANCY'S FRIENDS looked at her as if she had lost her mind.

"You can't go in that cave," Zoe warned her. "It would be suicide."

"She's right," Mick said firmly. "It's bad enough that those people have two hostages. Don't make it three, Nancy."

"I'm not going to march in there. We're going to swim in—through Kea Lake," said Nancy.

Theo's mouth dropped open. "That's right—we can use the underwater passage!" he cried.

Nancy stood up and began to search through the boat's compartments. At last she found what she wanted. "This will help," she said, pulling out a flare gun. "I have a plan that might give George and Kevin a chance to get away. But I'll need everyone's help."

Her friends were openly skeptical at first, but once Nancy explained her plan, they agreed to try it. Bess and Zoe had discovered a box of snorkeling gear belowdeck. And Theo found a chart of Dragonisi, which they could use to map out their plan. Within minutes the group was ready for action.

Theo and Mick would dive into the pond on the other side of the point and snorkel into the terrorists' cave, ending up in Kea Lake inside the large chamber. While Nancy used the flare gun to distract the terrorists, Mick and Theo would emerge from Kea Lake, free George and Kevin, and guide them out through the underwater passage.

"We'll bring along extra snorkeling gear for George and Kevin to use on the way out," said Mick.

"This pond will lead us to the tunnel of water," Theo said, pointing to a spot on the chart. "It's on the next beach, just beyond that stone ridge." Nancy looked up at the rocky point to the right of the terrorists' cave, then nodded.

Nancy turned to Bess and Zoe. "You should wait on the other side of the point for Theo and Mick to return with George and Kevin," Nancy explained. "And while you're waiting, watch for the police. Then come back for me."

"But what if the terrorists come after you?" Mick asked, his jaw tense.

"I can hide in that rocky section of the point, just like we did last time," Nancy assured him.

"Wait a minute," Bess objected as Theo guided the boat toward the rocks just out of sight of the terrorists' cave. "This sounds too risky to me."

"We've got to do it!" Nancy said, squeezing Bess's arm. "George and Kevin's lives depend on it." Nancy had put the flare gun and extra flares in a tote bag she found belowdeck. Now she slung the bag over her shoulder and descended the boat's ladder. As she carefully stepped into the waist-deep water, she held the bag over her head.

Fortunately, the beach was deserted as Nancy waded ashore and ran behind a clump of rocks. Turning, she saw the boat with her friends disappear beyond the jagged coastline. Momentarily she felt deserted. But then she concentrated on the task at hand.

Nancy looked at her watch. Ten minutes until the deadline, she thought. As she watched the minutes tick away on her watch, she mapped out her next move.

Five minutes later she decided that Mick and Theo were probably ready. Gritting her teeth, Nancy raced across the sandy dunes to the mouth of the tunnel.

Her progress was slowed as she plunged into darkness, but she inched forward, trying to remember the cave's layout from the day she and Mick had explored it. Her thundering heartbeat filled her ears as she moved on. Finally she turned a corner and saw the sunlit entrance of the inner chamber.

Holding her breath, she flattened herself against the stone wall and peered inside. George and Kevin were sitting against a huge boulder, bound together with rope. The three terrorists were sitting in a circle nearby, talking.

Nancy backed away and took out the flare gun. It's now or never, she thought. Bracing herself, she aimed the gun into the air and fired.

A red-tailed rocket whooshed through the darkness and shot into the rocky chamber. Confused shouts came from the cave as Nancy quickly reloaded the flare gun and fired again. Then she spun around and hurried through the dark tunnel toward the beach. She could hear the voices of the terrorists behind her—they were chasing her! She only hoped that she could lure all three of them out, leaving George and Kevin alone and unguarded for the rescue.

She stumbled, her arm scraping against the rough wall of the tunnel. Keep going! she urged herself on, just as she heard a loud pop and saw sparks fly off the cave wall ahead of her.

That's a ricocheting bullet! Nancy's feet pounded on the path. When she reached the mouth of the cave, she raced across the beach and dived behind a nearby pile of boulders. Her heart was pounding, but there was no time to catch her breath. She crouched on her knees in the sand, reloaded, and shot another flare toward the cave.

The shot was answered by a loud scream. Nancy peered over the top of the rock to see Mashti and Shara lingering at the mouth of the cave.

But where was the third terrorist—Rashid? She had to lure him out of the cave! Otherwise, Mick and Theo would receive a violent reception when they emerged from Lake Kea.

Just then Mashti aimed his gun in her direction and fired. Nancy ducked, her head hitting the sand as the bullet zinged overhead.

She was still taking cover when she felt the sand shift beside her. She had company. A hand closed over her shoulder, chilling her to the bone.

Chapter

Seventeen

STRONG FINGERS gripped Nancy's shoulder, pulling her up to a sitting position. Rashid! her mind screamed.

Nancy glared at the man—then let out a sigh of relief. It wasn't Rashid after all. She was staring into the surprised face of Officer Rossolatos. He didn't look at all pleased to see her.

"Nancy Drew!" he said, crouching beside her. "What are you doing here?"

"Trying to lure the terrorists out of the cave," she said desperately. They both pressed against a boulder as two more bullets flew overhead. Quickly she explained the plan she and her friends had put into action when it seemed that the police wouldn't arrive in time.

"We were held up waiting for the female agent," the officer explained.

Peering over the top of the huge rock, Nancy frowned. "I've got to get the other man out of the cave—or my friends will be in big trouble!"

"Say no more," Rossolatos said, kneeling beside her. He drew a gun from the holster at his waist and fired. Nancy cringed at the noise, but the barrage of shots sent Mashti and Shara scrambling behind the *Sea Star*.

But what about Rashid? Nancy thought frantically. It was a long shot, but she decided to shoot off one more flare. Quickly she reloaded the gun, stepped beside the boulder, and shot a flare toward the mouth of the cave.

The flare made it inside the entrance, and an echoing blast followed. A moment later Nancy saw Rashid crawl out of the cave entrance. He was firing a machine gun!

Nancy dived for cover, silently praying that the plan had worked. Behind her, half a dozen boats closed in on the shoreline. Rossolatos was speaking into a walkie-talkie, updating the other police and Interpol officers.

A shower of gunfire tore along the beach, chasing Rashid and ripping holes into the hull of the boat where Shara and Mashti were hiding. The terrorists were clearly outnumbered.

Within minutes the threesome surrendered, marching onto the open beach with their hands over their heads. Nancy watched as they were handcuffed and loaded onto a police boat.

Weak with relief, Nancy dropped the flare gun in the sand. "I need to find out if my friends made it out," she told Officer Rossolatos, anxiously pointing toward the rocky ridge. "Can one of the police boats give me a lift?"

Nancy was escorted onto a launch, which sped over the water, circling the point. Immediately she spotted the borrowed fishing boat anchored in the cove. Zoe and Bess were pacing along the beach.

"Still no sign of them," Zoe reported as Nancy waded ashore. "What was all that gunfire?"

When Nancy told them what had happened, Bess widened her eyes in terror. "Oh, Nancy, what if they don't make it!"

"They *will*," Nancy said, hugging Bess. She only hoped she was right!

The three girls waited in silence, staring into the clear pond that disappeared into the tunnel. Minutes dragged on, and Nancy thought the waiting would never end. Then, at last, she saw the silhouettes of swimmers coming through the dark mouth of the rock tunnel.

"It's George!" Bess squealed. "And Kevin! They're back!" She raced into the pond.

A moment later George and Kevin emerged from the water, pushing back their snorkel masks. Their clothes were clinging to them, but to Nancy, it was the best sight she had seen in her life.

"You had me scared sick!" Bess said, throwing her arms around her cousin.

Nancy was right behind Bess. "Thank goodness you're safe!" she said, hugging George and Kevin. Then she turned to Mick and Theo, who were just emerging from the water and taking off their masks.

"You guys are true heroes," Nancy said. She squeezed Theo's arm and gave Mick a big kiss.

"We can't take all the glory," Mick said, gazing down into Nancy's eyes. "We wouldn't have been able to get them out if you hadn't had the guts to go into the cave with that flare gun."

"That was amazing," George agreed. "One minute we were sitting there, doomed. The next minute there were rockets zipping through the cave."

"Thanks for saving us, guys," Kevin told the group. "After this I'll be happy to get back to the tame world of a TV sports announcer."

"After this week we'll all be ready for something tame," Bess said.

"Well," Theo said, folding his arms, "is anyone interested in some snorkeling lessons?"

Officer Rossolatos had asked the teens to remain on the scene until the police report was complete. Relieved that the terrorists had been captured, the group didn't mind hanging around.

At one point Nancy noticed George and Kevin stealing off for a private moment. A few minutes later they hugged, then separated. Kevin joined Mick and Theo, who were talking with Officer Rossolatos. George came over and sat next to Nancy on a boulder in the shade.

"Looks like you two were having a heart-to-heart," Nancy told her friend.

"About our relationship," George admitted, sitting down beside Nancy.

"And . . .?" Nancy prodded.

There was a thoughtful expression in George's brown eyes as she cupped her chin in her hands. "You know that Kevin has to report to Madrid on Sunday, right?"

Nancy nodded.

"Well," George continued, "his job keeps him on the road a lot. It's been bugging me for a while. I think we both need to be free to see other people." She let out a sigh. "I'm nuts about Kevin—you know that. But he's going to be on assignment in Europe for quite a while. I just think that we both need our freedom right now."

"How's Kevin taking it?" Nancy asked gently.

George shrugged. "He's not crazy about the idea, but he understands."

Nancy nodded sympathetically. The news of George's decision reminded Nancy that she faced a huge choice of her own. And suddenly her decision was crystal clear.

"Mail call!" Zoe shouted as she ran down the path to the hotel beach. It was Saturday morning, and Nancy and her friends had decided to spend the day lazing around at the inn. Theo, George, and Kevin were windsurfing just offshore, and Nancy, Mick, and Bess were stretched out on beach towels.

"Two letters from the States," Zoe said, handing envelopes to Nancy and Bess.

"News from the homefront," Bess said, tearing open a letter from her mother.

When Nancy saw the return address on her letter, she decided to read it later. She tucked it into her tote bag.

It was from Ned. No matter what the letter said, Nancy knew that Ned was only part of the reason for her decision not to marry Mick. Her adventures in Europe had taught her one important thing about herself: She thrived on independence. Marriage involved a commitment—a giant step that she wasn't ready to take. Right now she needed to be free to explore everything life had to offer.

The only bad part was that she had really fallen for Mick.

Nancy looked up as Zoe and Bess jumped up and ran into the water. Now that she and Mick were alone, she knew it was time to tell him what was on her mind.

"We need to talk," she told him, sitting up.

"Fire away," Mick said. He propped himself up on his elbows and faced her.

"About getting married," Nancy began, then paused when a rush of emotion nearly overwhelmed her. Tears stung her eyes as she looked over at Mick. "I—I'm just not ready, Mick. I'm crazy about you, but I'm not ready to make that kind of commitment, and leave my friends and father and—"

151

"Shhh," Mick whispered, gently placing a finger over Nancy's lips. "You don't have to explain. I understand."

He stared into Nancy's eyes for a moment, stroking her cheek. "I have to admit, I wish it weren't so. The door is always open, Nancy. Remember that. I'll never forget you." He reached into his knapsack and pulled out his wallet. Opening it, he showed Nancy a picture. "See?"

It was the photo Dimitri had taken of them the day they had arrived on Mykonos.

"It's a picture of us—and not a very good one," Nancy teased.

"What do you mean?" Mick said, taking a closer look at the photo. "I look spectacular!"

Just then everyone charged onto the beach and dragged Nancy and Mick into the water. A water battle ensued. Finally Nancy, Bess, and George managed to untangle themselves and head for the beach, leaving the others in the water.

"We noticed some heavy conversation going on," Bess said as she toweled off. "Did you decide about getting married?"

Nancy took a deep breath, then told her best friends about her decision.

"Wow," George said. "I mean, I'm glad you're not moving to the other side of the planet, but are you sure you're all right?"

"Don't feel bad, you two," Bess said, throwing her arms around Nancy and George.

Nancy smiled weakly. "Even though I know

it's the right choice, it will still be hard to say goodbye," she said.

"I know what you mean," George agreed.

"But soon we'll be back in the States," Bess pointed out. "And there's just something irresistible about All-American guys. . . ."

Nancy's next case:

While in San Francisco to visit Ned's cousin, whose husband works at one of the West Coast's hottest talent agencies, Nancy and Ned rub elbows with some of the city's most beautiful people. But one of those beautiful people has met a blunt and ugly end. The agency's number one model is out of the picture for good—found dead in a back alley!

The urge to make it big in front of the camera is powerful and tempting. Even Ned has stars in his eyes, and Nancy's beginning to wonder if he's lost sight of her. But behind the spotlight, she finds that the climb to the top can prove slippery and dangerous. Greed, ambition, and deceit are the rules of the game . . . and murder has struck the final pose . . . in *A TALENT FOR MUR DER*, Case #75 in the Nancy Drew Files™.